A GOOD GIRL & A DOWN SOUTH MILLIONAIRE 2

MICHELLE ELAINE

Cole Hart
SIGNATURE NOVELS

A Good Girl & A Down South Millionaire 2

Copyright © 2020 by Michelle Elaine

Published by Cole Hart Signature, LLC.

Mailing List

To stay up to date on new releases, plus get information on contests, sneak peeks, and more,

Go To The Website Below...

www.colehartsignature.com

THANK YOU

Cole Hart
SIGNATURE NOVELS

To our loyal Cole Hart Signature readers,

Cole Hart Signature is always growing and changing. Some of you have been following Cole Hart since the beginning of his career, while others have seen us go from Cole Hart Presents to Cole Hart Signature. Then there are our daily new supporters who've only known us for what we are as a company today. Despite our changes, how or when you became a fanatic, we want to kindly thank you for the support.

We appreciate all our Cole Hart Readers because without every single one of you, we wouldn't be the company we are today.

If this book is your first introduction to our company, welcome! And be sure to sign up for email list by going to Cole Hart Signature's website, and joining out text-mail list by texting ColeHartSig to (855)231-5230. Cole Hart Signature also has a Facebook group where fans get to discuss the plot, characters, overall releases about their favorite book. If itching for new and interesting conversation, join our Facebook group, Cole Hart Signature Readers Group!

Lastly, Cole Hart Signature is always interested in partnering with aspiring authors, new or experienced, who thrive in the African Urban Fiction and Romance Fiction genre. If you're interested in joining our team, go to www. colehartsignature.com/submissions.

Once again, we truly appreciate all the support over the years.

Much Love,
    CHS

JADA

I looked around my kitchen at the empty bottles of wine and shook my head. Vanessa would be on my case in a major way if she saw the way I had been living the past few weeks. I grabbed another bottle of white wine and a clean glass before heading to my balcony. I opened the door and stepped into the warm, night May air and took a seat at the patio table. I took in a deep breath and observed my surroundings in a desperate attempt to relax. The last several months had brought me my fair share of stress. I didn't want to feel any of that at the moment. I didn't want to feel anything. I set the wine and my glass down next to my ashtray and then grabbed my blunt and a lighter. I was raising the lit blunt to my lips as my phone started to ring. I rolled my eyes when I saw that my best friend, Vanessa Fowler, was attempting to reach me.

"Hello," I reluctantly answered.

"Hey, Jada," she greeted me evenly. "We're over here at Cameron's place getting ready to leave for the club. He wants to know if you're coming."

"If Cameron wants to know so badly, why didn't he call me?" I asked.

"He's busy … and I wanted to know too," Vanessa said. "You've been cooped up in your place for weeks. Come out with us tonight."

"Yeah. I don't think so. I don't really feel like it."

"Jada … everybody is coming out. You know you always have a good time at Compound, and it's Shannon's birthday," Vanessa tried to reason. "It will help you get back into the swing of things."

"Did you ever stop to think that maybe I don't want to get back into the swing of things?"

Vanessa released a heavy sigh. Our relationship had been strained for several weeks. "Jada, I know it's been an awful couple of months for you. Deuce's death and the miscarriage really got you down," she commented. "All of our lives have changed. I just want things to get back to normal … and you haven't been yourself in quite some time. I miss my friend."

"Maybe you should have thought about that before your inserted yourself in the middle of some business that didn't concern you," I told her.

Vanessa sighed heavily.

"Jesus! Again with this shit. I've apologized numerous times, Jada. It may not have been my place to tell Israel about your pregnancy, but he needed to know."

"All you did was further mess up an already messed up situation. You told my business, and then I still didn't hear from him. Do you know how much worse that made me feel that even after he knew I was pregnant he still didn't reach out to me?"

Vanessa was silent. I inhaled deeply on the blunt. I released a thick cloud of smoke from my lips before I spoke again.

"Look … I'm tired of having the same conversation with you. In order to move on we are probably going to have to agree to disagree and leave that situation in the past," I said. "I'm not going to make any promises, but I'll see if I can make it. I was supposed to be having drinks with Ayanna tonight. I'll let you know after that."

Vanessa was hesitant but responded, "Okay, Jada. I'll talk to you later."

I ended the call and placed the phone on the table and poured a glass of wine. I inhaled another deep breath of fresh air as I looked down onto the city of Atlanta. I took a long sip of wine as the late May breeze whipped through my hair. I looked down at the spaghetti-strapped tank and boy shorts I was wearing and took another sip from my glass.

I had told Vanessa a lie.

I did not have plans to meet up with my sister Ayanna, and I certainly did not feel like going to anybody's club. As a matter of fact, I did not feel like leaving the comfort of my condo at all. Vanessa's words had been true. In the past few months, I had lost my older brother and two childhood friends, one of whom had left behind a pregnant girlfriend. In addition to that, I suffered a painful miscarriage shortly after the love of my life and my child's father, Israel Mann, ended our relationship for good and moved back to Houston, TX where he was playing professional football.

After finishing my blunt and my glass of wine, I reached for the bottle and poured another full glass. As soon as I took the first sip, my cell phone started to ring again. It was my younger brother, Cameron. I hesitantly answered right before it went to voicemail.

"Yo," Cameron spoke.

"What's up?" I asked evenly.

"Ness said you ain't coming out tonight," Cameron replied. "What's up with that, Big Sis?"

I rolled my eyes. Vanessa just couldn't keep her damn mouth shut. "That's not what I said, Cam. I –"

"I know what you said, Jay. I think you forgot that Vanessa knows you as well as I do so she knows when you're lying," he said as he cut me off. "She also knows that Yanni is still in Charleston visiting Tony's family."

I was quiet.

"Look, sis. I didn't lose a baby, so I'm not going to pretend that I know how you feel about that or about Israel skipping town on you," he said, "but I lost a brother too. So, you ain't the only one feeling that pain. I'm not saying that you have to stay out all night with us, but its Shannon's birthday. Just come show that pretty face of yours. Please."

Cameron always had a way of getting through to me, especially when no one else could. Throughout our adult years, he had become more than just a brother to me. He was one of my best friends.

"Okay. I'll be there," I hesitantly answered.

"Good."

"Alright."

"See you in a few."

"Bye Cameron."

"Jada ..."

"What?"

"If you're not there by midnight, I will drive to that pretty little condo of yours and drag your ass down here myself."

"Alright. Damn! Let me go take a shower!"

Cameron laughed as I ended the call. After finishing off my glass, I headed back to my master suite to get ready for my night out.

Thirty minutes later, I was pulling on an all-white Herve Leger bandage dress. I had already applied my makeup, and I was wearing my hair in its naturally curly state. I was inside of my walk-in closet stepping into my Christian Louboutin heels when I heard my phone beep alerting me that I had received a text message. I walked back into my bedroom and grabbed my cell phone off of my bed.

Message received: "Hey ..."

It was from Israel Mann – my ex-boyfriend and the father of the baby I miscarried a few months prior. I quickly deleted the message and tossed the phone back onto my bed before I finished putting on my jewelry. Twenty minutes later, I was stepping into my Mercedes-Benz truck. When I arrived at the club it was fifteen minutes before midnight. I bypassed a long line of people waiting to get into the club and walked right up to the entrance.

"Ms. Reid," the bouncer greeted me with a smile.

"Raymond," I greeted him with a smile of my own as he stepped to the side and let me enter the building.

It had been a number of months since I was in anybody's club, and I wasn't sure if I was ready to be out that night either. However, I had shown up to support my family. Family had always been important to me. I just hoped that the night went off without any drama. I took a deep breath and smoothed down the front of my dress as I headed straight to VIP in search of my family.

I was greeted with warm hugs when I approached my crew. Shannon, Cameron's girlfriend and the birthday girl, made her way towards me and hugged me tightly.

"Cam mentioned earlier that you might not be feeling up to coming out," she said, "but I'm really glad that you made it. With everything that's happened in the last few months, it means a lot to me that you are here. Now, it's time to party and just have a good time. Your brother has spent a lot of money on a lot of alcohol to make sure that we all enjoy ourselves tonight."

Shannon and I shared a laugh.

"I can see that," I said as I looked at the various bottles of alcohol in our section. "I'm already glad I came out. I wanted to help you bring in your birthday. The alcohol is just an added bonus."

We laughed again. A few seconds later, we were interrupted by Vanessa as she approached us.

"I'm so happy you made it!" Vanessa squealed, wrapping an arm around my shoulders.

I narrowed my eyes at her. "You know why I'm here," I said.

"Huh?" Vanessa asked, taking a sip of the drink in her hand.

I rolled my eyes. "I know that your loudmouth snitched on me to Cam," I said to Vanessa before turning back towards Shannon. "What does my brother have for us to drink? ... and where the hell is Cameron?"

"We've got all types of bottles here," Shannon said as she pointed to the array of alcohol on the table. "Both brown and clear so pick your poison. As for your brother, girl, who knows? I think he ran into someone, and they started talking business. He should be back over here in a little bit."

I nodded and started to fix a drink while Shannon made her way back over to a few of her other friends. With cranberry juice and whiskey in my cup, I sat down on one of the nearby couches. Vanessa sat down next to me.

"Did you really have to front me out to Cam?" I asked.

"Did you really have to lie about your plans this evening?" Vanessa countered.

I shrugged my shoulders but took a sip of my drink instead of responding. "So, guess who texted me while I was trying to get ready to leave the house?"

"Who?"

"Israel."

"What?"

"Exactly," I responded as I shook my head and ran my fingers through my thick, curly hair.

"Seriously ... you guys haven't spoken since he left for Houston. Not even after I told him about the baby or the miscarriage. What the hell did he have to say now?" Vanessa questioned with a frown.

"That's the thing, girl. He sends me a one word text message that says 'hey'. What the hell? I deleted that shit!" I answered with a frown.

Vanessa shook her head as we both continued to sip on our drinks. After a few moments, she said, "Jay, you know I've always been Israel's biggest fan ... but I don't know anymore. Everything is just so different now. After everything that has happened and all that you two have been through, he has the nerve to send you a one-word text message after moving halfway across the country on you over two months ago. That's some bullshit."

I sucked back the rest of my drink and nodded. "Yeah. I absolutely agree," I responded as I stood up to pour myself another drink. "I don't have any words for him, Ness. Not right now, and probably not ever. I'm done with him and all that drama. I'm sick of it."

"As you should be," Vanessa quickly added. "Forget all that shit, and let's have a good time tonight. Ain't nobody worried about his ass."

I laughed as I raised my glass. "I'll drink to that."

AARON

There was no doubt that Compound was the place to be on any given Saturday night, but it was particularly packed that night. It was a little before one in the morning and the crowd was thick. I gave a friendly nod to a business associate I passed on my way to VIP. I was looking for a group of friends who arrived well before me. As I navigated my way through the crowd, I ran into one of the club's main promoters.

"Ay yo Jake, what's good?" I asked as I slapped hands with him.

"Ain't shit man. Same shit just a different Saturday," he said with a grin. "It's good to see you in town though."

"It's good to be here, man. It's always good to be in the A," I said with a smile as I rubbed my hands together. "I make a lot of money in the A."

Jake laughed heartily and nodded. "Ay, I feel you on that," he said. "Well I know you're here trying to get up with your people, but let me know if you need anything, alright?"

"Definitely," I responded as I started to head back in the direction of my friends.

Before I could walk away my attention was captured by one of the most attractive women I had seen in a long time. With the dim lights in the club, I could only imagine how perfect her angelic face would look in the daylight. From what I could see, the white form-fitting dress was hugging every curve of her voluptuous frame. I couldn't wait to get a little closer to see what she was really working with. In a split second, I knew that I had to have her.

"Aye Jake!" I called his attention before he got too far away.

"What's up?"

"Lil mama in the white ... the one with the large group and all those bottles," I said. "Yo, who the hell is that?"

Jake scratched his head and his forehead wrinkled in confusion. "You talking about Jada?"

I shrugged my shoulders. "Whatever her name is, she's bad as hell. I gotta get her, bruh. You know her?"

"Yeah," Jake answered. "I'm surprised that you don't know her. That's –"

"I don't care who she is or who she's with. She's mine tonight," I said as I continued to watch her body sway to the beat of the song that was playing.

After parting ways with Jake, I flagged down a waitress and sent a couple bottles of champagne over to the pretty chick in the white dress and her friends. I eventually found my best friend, Lucas Malone, seated at a table by himself. I approached the table and sat down across from him.

"Where's everyone else?" I asked.

Luke shrugged his shoulders. "They're somewhere around here enjoying the party."

"That's cool," I said. "You're the main one I was trying to catch up with anyway."

"So, I'm guessing that means I can finally get some answers," Luke stated. "Like, why are we here?"

"In the club?"

Luke shook his head. "Nah, man. In Atlanta. You never told me what this trip was about. You just said to come up here with you for a few weeks, but we never really stay up here that long."

I pulled my eyes away from the woman I sent the champagne to and made direct eye contact with my right-hand man. "I'll fill you in when there's more to tell. I don't really have all the details myself. I have a meeting set up for tomorrow, and then I'll be able to tell you more," I answered honestly.

Luke's facial expression told me that he wasn't completely satisfied with my answer. "Black, I hear you, but if something major is going to go down I would like to know sooner rather than later."

I took a sip of my beer and nodded. "Luke, come on, man. I have never led you astray. Just trust me. When there's more to tell, I promise you will be the first to know."

I was speaking to Luke, but I had turned my attention back to the woman in the body-hugging white dress. She and her friends accepted the bottles of champagne and were drinking and dancing along to the music. Out the corner of my eye, I could see Luke roll his eyes and shake his head when he noticed that my attention was somewhere else.

Luke and a few of our associates made it to Atlanta the day before. Needing to take care of a few things back home in Miami, I didn't make it to Atlanta until a few hours before arriving at the club. We were supposed to meet to discuss business, but as the men were spread throughout the club, I knew that our conversation would have to wait until a later date. My father, Emmanuel "Manny" Mercer was the head of the Ramirez Cartel, major drug distributors and crime organization that originated in the Dominican Republic many years ago. Manny, who was African American, had risen to the top of the organization after winning the heart of my mother, Sophia Ramirez Mercer, and the trust of her father, my grandfather, Alejandro Ramirez. After decades as the head of the family business and health complications, Alejandro decided to retire and turn everything over to my father. In the beginning, there was friction amongst the family since there had never been someone who was not of blood relation to be in charge. However, my father had proven to be a sound choice and had been very successful, bringing in more money to the Cartel in the fifteen years that he had been in charge than Alejandro had ever made.

As the only son and the heir to the throne, I was being groomed to one day take over my father's position. Being the first and second in command of an international drug operation, my father and I were pulling money in from different states and countries. However, Miami was where we both maintained permanent residency. Luke and the other men in the club with me that night also lived in Miami, which was why he was questioning our current trip. It wasn't unusual for me to travel to Atlanta. However, my trips never lasted that long, and I did not normally bring a team with me. Luke was trying to get the truth about what was really going on.

"Just make sure I get that call tomorrow, Black," he said as he took another sip of his drink.

"I got you," I told my friend.

Regardless of how hard Luke pried, I wasn't willing to give up any answers. Not yet. He would have to wait until tomorrow. For now, I was purely focused on the woman that had captured my attention. She and her friends were obviously having a good time. They continued to sing along and dance to the music. It did not take them long to empty the bottles of champagne. They were accompanied earlier by a group of men, but for the moment the women were alone.

It was time for me to make my move.

I stood up and told Luke, "I'll be right back."

I walked away from the table and started to navigate my way through the crowded VIP area. I was halfway towards my destination when I was stopped by an all too familiar face.

"Well, well, well; look who it is," Kara Ross said as she smiled in my face and pressed her body against mine. "I had no idea you were back in town."

"A lot of people don't know," I said nonchalantly, while I looked past her towards the woman who held my attention.

"So, what's up?" Kara asked with a seductive smile and her hands on her waist.

I looked down at her and tried to hide the disdain from my face. She was a mistake I repeated one too many times in the not so distant past. Kara was a former stripper turned video model with an amazing body and an even better-looking face. However, she was annoying and way too clingy for the casual situation we once shared. She was younger than most women I entertained, and her immaturity had eventually turned me off of our little situation.

"What do you mean?" I asked.

"I mean ... what's up with me and you?" she asked, licking her bottom lip and rubbing my shoulder. "You trying to come by my place after you leave here?"

Hell no.

"Nah. I gotta early start in the morning," I lied, "but I'll hit you up some time, though."

I quickly stepped around Kara and walked towards the woman I had been eyeing since my arrival. The white dress looked like it had been painted onto her shapely frame. I stared at her round behind and toned legs while I marveled at how narrow her waist was. For a moment, I just stood and watched as she moved her hips and bobbed her head to the music – her thick, curly hair was bouncing to the beat. I eventually approached her and tapped her on the shoulder.

"Yes?" she asked as she turned around to look at me expectantly.

I had to tear my eyes away from her cleavage, which was spilling out of the top of her dress.

"Excuse me ... I don't mean to interrupt, but I couldn't help but notice you from where I was sitting," I said, "and you're wearing the hell out of that dress."

"Thanks," she responded flatly and turned back towards her friends.

I smirked to myself and shook my head. It was rare that my advances were denied. I could tell that she was intoxicated, and that was fine. I wasn't trying to have a full-blown conversation with her. I honestly had other business I could be tending to, but I didn't want to walk away without at least getting her name and phone number. I tapped her shoulder again.

She spun around with a frown, but her facial expression softened when she looked into my eyes. "I'm sorry," she said. "Your face looks familiar. Do I know you?"

I smiled at her but shook my head. "Nah. I would definitely remember a face like yours," I told her, "but maybe you should get to me."

She raised an eyebrow but smiled as well. "Is that so?" she asked.

I nodded and watched her place her hand on her hip and take a step closer to me. My smile widened. I could tell from her body language and the look in her eyes that if I played my cards right, I would be getting much more than her phone number.

CAMERON

*M*y eyes slowly opened, and I tried to look around the dark room. My vision settled on my cell phone. I picked it up to see that not only was it almost four o'clock in the morning, but that I also had missed thirty-four calls. I scrolled through the call log to see that the majority of the calls were from Shannon. I shook my head and let out a heavy sigh before sitting my phone back down and closing my eyes. A brief moment later my eyes popped open again when the sleeping figure next to me turned on her side, her back towards me. It was not Shannon. I was lying on my back in another woman's bed while my girlfriend was presumably alone in our bed across town blowing my phone up.

I set up and swung my legs over the side of the queen-sized, four-post bed. I hung my head and released another deep sigh. I reached for my boxers and stepped into them before I stood up. Then I reached towards the bedside table and picked up my cell phone, my lighter, and the other half of my blunt from earlier in the evening. I stepped away from the bed and headed for the balcony where I closed the sliding glass door behind me. The city skyline of Atlanta was breathtaking, but it did nothing to relax my mind. I sparked the lighter and held it towards what was remaining of the blunt in my hand. However, there was no amount of alcohol or weed that could stop the thousands of thoughts that were running through my head. I had a billion and one problems that all needed solving, and I knew where I needed to start. With the blunt in one hand and my phone in the other, I dialed Shannon's cell phone.

"Hello," she answered with an attitude.

"Hey, baby," I said. "I just saw –"

Shannon cut me off before I could explain. "I was just making sure that you were alive."

Click.

I released a cloud of smoke from my lips and hesitated before dialing Shannon's number again.

"What?" she snapped.

"Shan, my phone was on silent. I really didn't know that you were trying to reach me," I told her.

"You left me at the club on my birthday! Did you think that I wasn't going to call?!" she screamed into the phone.

"Babe, I –"

"Uh-uh, don't 'babe' me!" I had never heard her so upset. "You told me that you were stepping out for a moment to take a phone call, and then you never came back. I had to catch a ride home with one of my girls. *What the fuck, Cameron?*"

"I know. I know," I said, as I tried to come up with an explanation. "Some stuff came up with PO and Zo. I kind of lost track of time. I know I should have called you earlier. I'm sorry I dipped out like that, but baby, believe me when I say that I wouldn't have left you with people that I didn't trust."

"So where are you now?"

"Huh?"

"It doesn't sound like you're in your car on the way home, and it's quiet wherever you are. Therefore, I know you are not with those loudmouth niggas you always run with," she stated. "Where are you?"

I hesitated. "Babe, I just –"

"Save it, Cameron," Shannon cut me off again. "Don't even waste your energy trying to come up with another lie. Like I said, I was just calling to make sure that you were okay. Clearly you are fine wherever you are, so just stay there. I don't want to see your face tonight."

Shannon hung up the phone again.

That went about as bad as I imagined it would.

I sucked my teeth and rolled my eyes. I was about to call Shannon back for a third time but stopped when I heard the sliding glass door open and close. I lowered my phone by my side and looked over my shoulder. I fought the urge to shake my head as Brianna Taylor made her way over to where I was standing. I smiled at the lingerie she was wearing. Even though she looked amazing, deep down I knew that going home with her that night had been a mistake. It wasn't the first time though. Brianna smiled at me and kissed me on the lips before she took the blunt from my hand and inhaled deeply before passing it back to me. She wrapped her arms around my neck and stepped closer to me, pressing her firm body against mine.

At five foot four, Brianna was almost an entire foot shorter than me. When I looked down at her and slid an arm around her narrow waist, I knew that there was no denying how beautiful she was. Brianna had a smooth, mahogany-colored complexion and thick, natural hair that touched her shoulders. I admired the twist out hairstyle that she was wearing. Her dark brown almond-shaped eyes complimented her full, heart-shaped lips. I marveled at her well-defined thighs and her firm behind. As much as I knew I should have been home with Shannon, I would have been lying if I did not admit that just the sight of Brianna turned me on. There was no denying our physical attraction to one another, and I couldn't keep my hands off of her.

"You sneaking out of bed in the middle of the night?" she jokingly asked me with a smile on her face.

I shook my head. "No, I just came out here to smoke ... and you looked like you were sleeping peacefully. I didn't want to disturb you."

"Oh," she said, "... 'cause I was about to say ... I know this fool ain't trying to creep out in the middle of the night."

"That didn't even cross my mind," I lied.

"Good," Brianna said. After a brief moment of silence passed between us, she said, "I'm going to head back inside. Finish your blunt and come back to bed."

I simply nodded in agreement.

"Because I'm not done with you yet," Brianna said as she slipped her hands inside of my boxers, "and from the feel of things you're not done with me either."

I watched as Brianna walked back into her bedroom. I thought about telling her that something had come up and that I needed to leave. However, I thought that would lead to further questioning from Brianna since it was four o'clock in the morning and most of my people were asleep at that time. I already had to deal with Shannon when I eventually made it back home. I didn't want to start an argument with Brianna too. I didn't want her to start getting suspicious. The current arrangement we shared was perfect. Neither Brianna nor Shannon knew about each other, and I intended to keep it that way. I finished what was left of my blunt and tossed the ashes off the side of the balcony. Then, I made my way into the bedroom and slipped back into Brianna's bed. I would have to find a way to apologize to Shannon later.

JADA

16

The sound of running water awakened me. Because I lived alone, I was confused to say the least. I was even more startled when I opened my eyes and realized that I was not at my place. Looking at the California King sized bed I was in and the expensive, tasteful decorations of the bedroom, I honestly had no idea where I was. The running water was coming from the shower in the adjoining bathroom. My eyes darted around the room as I looked for my belongings.

When the shower stopped, I was in full on panic mode. In only the nude-colored matching bra and thong I had worn the previous night, I pushed back the covers and hopped out of the bed. I darted towards the corner of the room where I saw my clutch purse laying on a chaise lounge. I froze when I heard footsteps enter the room.

"Good afternoon, Sleeping Beauty," I heard his deep voice say.

I slowly turned around and laid eyes on the sexiest man I had seen in a while. I quickly recognized him as the man who had approached me in the club when I was celebrating Shannon's birthday the previous night. He was tall with a caramel brown complexion that was smooth and even. He had a perfectly trimmed mustache and beard and his teeth were blindingly white. His wavy black shoulder length hair was still damp from his shower and pulled back into a low, thick ponytail. His piercing dark brown eyes and his half smile displayed a set of dimples that had me in a trance. Fresh out of the shower, he was standing before me in nothing but a towel. My eyes took in his broad shoulders and impeccably chiseled chest and abs, which highlighted his muscular, athletic physique. Tattoos covered both of his arms as well as his chest. My head slightly tilted to the side as I watched a few beads of water cascade from his chest down to the top of the crisp white towel that was wrapped around his waist. I shook my head to snap myself out of the daze that I was in.

"Afternoon?" I asked.

He laughed and walked over to a Louis Vuitton duffle bag on the floor that rested against one of the walls. "It's almost two o'clock in the afternoon," he answered as he grabbed a pair of boxer briefs from his bag.

He removed the towel from his waist and tossed it onto his bed. For a brief moment, he stood naked in front of me before stepping into his underwear. Instantly, I remembered our drunken rendezvous from the night before.

"Two o'clock? Damn …" I said quietly.

He didn't hear me and continued to pull clothes out of his duffle bag and get dressed. I stood awkwardly by the chaise lounge for a brief moment before I spoke again.

"Where are we?"

"My house," he answered with a smirk. "More specifically … we're in Sandy Springs."

I nodded in acknowledgment. The city of Sandy Springs was a suburb just north of the city of Atlanta. It wouldn't take me long to get back home. There were very few things I remembered from the previous night. I had no idea where my keys and clothes were or how I had gotten to the attractive stranger's home.

"Excuse me …"

"Aaron," he answered, as he tightened the belt on the jeans he was wearing.

"I'm sorry, Aaron," I said. "Do you know where my keys and my clothes are?"

"Yeah," he answered as he disappeared into his walk-in closet. He returned a few moments later with my shoes in one hand and my dress on a hanger in his other hand. He placed the shoes down on the floor and laid the dress across the bed. "I put your stuff up. I know how particular some women can be about their designer labels, and I know this shit ain't cheap."

I didn't respond. I walked back over to his bed and quickly

slipped into the dress. Aaron sat down on the edge of his bed and tied the laces on the white Christian Louboutin sneakers he had stepped into. After putting on my dress, I stepped into my heels.

"My keys?"

"Oh! Yeah, your home girl drove your whip home," he said nonchalantly. He grabbed his wallet and stuck it in his back pocket.

My forehead wrinkled in confusion. "What?" I asked. "Who drove my car where? And how did I get here?"

Aaron walked over to where I was standing leaving little to no room between our bodies. Even in my heels, he still towered over me. "Your girl ... the pretty brown-skinned one with the high cheekbones. She drove your car. She said she would get up with you sometime today. You rode with me over here."

I squeezed my eyes shut and shook my head in disbelief. "How drunk was I last night?"

"Damn, it's like that?" Aaron questioned with a frown.

"You're attractive and all, and I'm sure last night was fun," I started, "but I don't know you. I don't let other people drive my car, and I sure as hell don't make a habit of riding anywhere with strangers."

Aaron looked directly into my brown eyes. In a low tone with a slick smile he said, "You sure didn't seem to mind riding last night."

I did a double take. I wanted to cuss him out or slap him or something ... but I didn't. He was standing so close to me that my breasts were brushing against his well-defined torso with each breath that I took. His presence was powerful and unnerving at the same time. I was at a complete loss for words.

I took a step back and quietly asked, "Can you just take me home, please?"

"Certainly," he answered. "Come on."

Aaron grabbed my hand and led me out of the room. I

wanted to snatch my hand back, but I didn't. My eyes wandered around as I followed him down the hallway to a large, elaborate staircase. I couldn't deny that the house was beautifully extravagant. Given the location and appearance, I estimated the house to be right around a million dollars. Instead of heading out the front door, Aaron walked into the kitchen. I spotted an attractive middle-aged Hispanic woman stocking groceries in a large stainless-steel refrigerator.

"Mr. Mercer, will you be back for dinner?" she asked.

I didn't miss the dirty look the woman threw my way.

Aaron shrugged his shoulders. "Probably not, Lissa," he answered. "If I am, I'll probably just grab something on my way in. As a matter of fact, once you finish up here you can go on and head out for the day."

"Okay, Mr. Mercer," she answered, cutting her eyes towards me again.

AARON APPEARED TO BE OBLIVIOUS TO OUR EXCHANGE, BUT I rolled my eyes at his housekeeper. Taking me by the hand, Aaron led me into the three-car attached garage. My eyes rested on the three cars before me: a midnight blue Maserati, a steel gray Aston Martin, and a white 7 series BMW. He walked to the passenger side of the BMW and opened the door for me.

"Hop in."

Silently, I slid into the passenger seat. After giving him my address, he took off towards my condo. We made small talk and listened to the radio during the drive to my place. From his house to the cars in his garage, it was obvious that Aaron had money, but I wasn't interested in digging into his personal business. I just wanted to get home and take a shower. Wanting to avoid the dreaded walk of shame through the visitors' entrance to my building, I gave him the gate code to the parking deck so I could enter the building more discreetly. Aaron pulled into a parking space near an entrance to the building and shut the engine off.

"You could've kept it running," I said while reaching for the door handle. "I wasn't planning on inviting you in."

Aaron laughed. "Your mouth has no filter."

I shrugged my shoulders.

"305-555-8824."

"What is that?" I asked.

"That's my phone number," Aaron said to me. "Answer the phone when I call you later."

"I didn't give you my number."

"You did," he answered. "You don't remember much at all. Do you?"

I shrugged my shoulders and said, "Maybe you weren't worth remembering."

Aaron laughed heartily and shook his head at me.

"Now you know that's a damn lie. There's a wet spot in my bed right now that will prove how much you enjoyed yourself," he said. "As much as your smart mouth is a turn on, I don't have time to finish anything you're trying to start right now. You already said you weren't inviting me in, and I have somewhere else I need to be anyway. Just answer the phone when I call you later."

"And why would I do that?" I asked as I opened the door to exit his car.

"Shit, I don't know. Maybe I might want to take your mean ass out to dinner or something," he answered with a laugh before turning the engine back on. "Pick up the phone when I call, and I guess you'll find out."

I shook my head and rolled my eyes while I got out of the car. Stepping away from the car, I noticed that Aaron was waiting until I made it inside my building before pulling off. He had a look of confidence on his face like he was certain he would be seeing me again.

. . .

JULIAN

I sat alone in the back corner of the Houston's restaurant. Throughout the years, it had always been a habit that in public I would sit where no one could approach me from behind. I looked down at the watch on my wrist. My company was scheduled to arrive at any moment. I glanced at a nearby window and spotted a woman walking down the street that reminded me so much of my late wife, Carmen, that I had to look away.

It had been five years since Carmen's passing, and I was still trying to find a way to deal with the grief. At the time of her death, I naturally took on the role of being the rock of the family. I had remained stone-faced and was the support system for my children, especially Cameron and Jada as they dealt with the loss of their mother. Immediately after her funeral, it was back to business as usual where I continued to make sure that my presence was felt in the streets so that my money and my family were well taken care of. For the past five years, I had been going full steam ahead continuing to expand my empire and becoming one of the most well-known and respected businessmen in the area, both legally and illegally.

However, with the death of Deuce, my eldest child, I realized that I needed a break. I was dealing with the feelings of loss and grief that I had not stopped to acknowledge five years earlier. I had worked my entire adult life to make sure that both my family and my finances were secure, but in the process, I had ended up losing two of the people closest to me. I desperately needed to refocus. With the recent news that my mother was diagnosed with cancer, I needed to get away from Atlanta. That was the exact reason I called the meeting I was scheduled to have. I was planning to take some much-needed time away from the criminal enterprise I spent over three decades building.

The natural thing would have been to turn the family business over to family. However, in Deuce's absence, I wasn't sure if I could do that. Being a college graduate, my older daughter Ayanna had always been business-minded, but she did not have the street presence to handle my not so legal business ventures. I had always gone above and beyond to shelter her and my younger daughter, Jada, from my life in the streets. Ayanna managed to stay far away from the streets, but somehow Jada always found herself associated with my business associates. She continuously seemed to have her nose in and around my illegal affairs. She had done such an outstanding job running the family restaurant and a clothing boutique, that she and Ayanna were planning to open a salon and spa soon. Even still, I was not going to put my baby girl anywhere near my street business, especially with the issues she had been dealing with over the course of the past several months.

Then there was Cameron. He was the youngest of my children, but next to Deuce he would have been the likely replacement to follow in my footsteps. However, he had been having a rough couple of months, much like his sister Jada. Deuce and Cameron were extremely close, and Deuce's death had certainly taken a toll on him. Cameron had always been a hot head with a smart mouth, but his behavior lately had bordered on erratic. I hoped Cameron was just trying to process his grief as well. Yet and still, I knew that one ill thought out, costly mistake could cause my empire to come crumbling down.

That was not a risk I was willing to take.

Instead, I had a plan. In the interest of supporting Cameron as well as protecting my wealth and freedom, I called in a favor for help. I reached out to the only family besides my own that I fully trusted to help Cameron with the day to day of the business while I spent time with my mother in California. That was the purpose of the meeting today – to discuss my plans with the man who came to help. I looked at my watch once again and then looked to my right to see my company approaching my table.

"Hey Julian ... sorry for running a little behind. I kind of got a late start to my day."

I stood to greet him and the two of us slapped hands. "No problem," I said as we both took our seats. "I figured you might have gone out last night after you got in. You and your father always did enjoy the Atlanta nightlife."

Aaron Mercer laughed and nodded in agreement. "Oh yeah," he stated as he looked over the menu. "I definitely had a good time last night."

JADA

THREE MONTHS LATER

*S*unlight made its way into the large, master bedroom and shined onto my face. I slowly opened my eyes and shifted my head on the mound of pillows. A smile spread across my face when I noticed that Aaron's arm was still securely wrapped around my waist while he slept on his side, his chest pressed against my back. I released a pleased sigh and closed my eyes for a few more minutes.

I felt like I had been smiling for the past three months. Two days after we met, Aaron took me out for sushi, and we had been inseparable ever since. Countless dinner dates, weekends spent together, and even a couple quick getaways had taken place over the last ninety days. We had our hands full balancing our careers and our blossoming relationship, but I enjoyed every minute. Ayanna and I were busy preparing for the salon and spa we were opening in a few months. Aaron shared with me that he was a senior-level marketing executive for an Atlanta based firm but also revealed that his family had money. I turned to face him while he continued to sleep peacefully. Gently caressing his cheek, I softly kissed him on the lips before slipping out of bed. He was just what I needed in order to recover from Israel.

On my tip toes, I quietly made my way around the room, so I did not disturb my sleeping boyfriend. I pulled one of his V-neck white T-shirts out of his dresser and slipped it over my naked body. I stepped into my La Perla underwear and exited the bedroom. With my cell phone in my hand, I skipped down the stairs while searching for music on my phone. Once I was in the large, gourmet kitchen, I pulled my hair into a messy high ponytail and started to play my music while I began to prepare breakfast.

In the beginning, I tried very hard to resist my feelings for Aaron. I felt like he had shown up too soon after my split with Israel and way too soon after my miscarriage. I did not think that it was appropriate to become involved in anything serious. I tried to tell myself that with all the loss I had dealt with in the months prior that I was just looking for any source of comfort. Aaron had provided that and more. He had given me a sense of security and stability that I had not felt in years. It did not take long for him to break down the walls that I had put up. He found his way into my heart and got me to open up when I least expected it.

I hummed along to "Say You Will" by Brandy and stirred a pot of grits before turning the heat down on the stove. Barefoot, I danced along to the heartfelt ballad and made my way over to the stainless-steel refrigerator. I grabbed the carton of eggs and was turning back towards the granite kitchen island when Aaron's voice startled me.

"Do you enjoy cooking half naked?" he asked with a smile as he pulled a T-shirt on over his head. His wavy hair was loose and resting on his shoulders.

I laughed and looked down at the T-shirt and underwear I wore. "As much as you enjoy watching it," I answered, breaking a few eggs and putting them into a mixing bowl.

"Then you must love it," he said as he kissed me on the cheek. He walked around the kitchen island and sat down on one of the stools. "Where's Julissa? I thought she was supposed to be here today."

"She called while you were sleeping, and I told her that it would be okay if she didn't come in. I thought you and I could spend a little bit of time together today," I answered, while seasoning the eggs.

Aaron nodded and glanced at the time on the oven. It was almost noon.

"What did you have in mind?" he asked.

I shrugged my shoulders and poured the egg mixture into the skillet. I just wanted to spend time with him. It didn't matter what we did.

"I don't know. Movies … bowling … dinner?" I threw out a few suggestions.

Spotting the platter of cooked bacon and buttered toast, Aaron realized I was almost finished cooking. He went to a nearby cabinet and pulled down two plates.

"I have a meeting for work around three, but we can definitely do something after that."

I pouted.

"You have to go into work on a Saturday?"

Aaron nodded. "Yeah, mama. There are some changes going on in the office … but it shouldn't take too long."

I hated how busy he had become with work, but I loved the way he called me 'mama'.

"Good."

"I promise it will only take me a few hours but after that, I'm all yours," he stated as he smacked my behind.

I giggled as I started to fill our plates with food. A few minutes later, we sat at the kitchen island enjoying our food.

"Oh, I forgot to tell you that I've finally decided on birthday dinner plans," I stated between bites of food.

"Cool. What's the move?"

"We're going to dinner on Tuesday night. Eight-thirty at The Capital Grille."

Aaron nodded as he took a bite of his toast. "Sounds good."

"And just a reminder … my family is going to be there," I told him.

"Okay."

"Like … my father's whole side of the family except my grandma. My brother, sister, Dad, two of my aunts …"

"Okay," Aaron laughed.

He shrugged his shoulders.

I gave him a questioning look. "Is that okay with you?"

"Yeah," Aaron answered nonchalantly. "Why wouldn't it be?"

"I don't know," I answered as I looked down at my plate. "I just know how men can get when it's time to meet the family … and my family is pretty intense. Besides, it's been a very long time since I've brought someone new around them … and that didn't end well."

Aaron sat his fork down and looked at me. Avoiding eye contact with him, I pushed my grits around my plate with my fork.

"Hey … look at me," he said as he turned my face towards him. "Yeah, we both know that your last relationship was kinda fucked up, but all that shit's over now. I ain't going nowhere. What are you so worried about?"

I shrugged my shoulders. Aaron turned back towards his food and took another bite of his muffin.

"Besides," he said flashing me his usual half smile, "Families love me."

I laughed.

"Is that so?"

"Absolutely," he responded. "Plus, I already met Ayanna at your restaurant and won her over easily. You said she was the most intense one."

I laughed and nodded my head. "She is."

"Good. So, neither of us has anything to worry about," he stated. "You should start preparing for when I take you down to Miami to meet my people. My family is a handful."

"Hmmm ... a large, partially Hispanic loudmouth family," I stated. "I think I might have some experience in that department."

We both laughed.

"Aye ... hurry up and finish your food so you can join me in the shower before I head to this meeting," Aaron told me.

I winked my eye at him seductively and said, "You don't have to tell me twice."

JULIAN

I stood in front of the large bay window in my home office. I looked down at my front yard and the rest of my neighborhood and noticed that it was a lot quieter than I had anticipated it would be. For it to be Labor Day weekend, I expected to see a host of cars parked on the street from cookouts or kids playing in the street but didn't. Normally I would have had a house full of family members as well, since the Reid clan usually took advantage of every opportunity to spend time with one another. However, Ayanna was with her husband visiting his family in South Carolina, and my other two children had plans of their own. Besides, we would all be together for Jada's birthday dinner in a few days.

"Are you seriously just now telling Cameron about your plans?" PO's voice broke into my thoughts.

I looked over my shoulder at one of my most trusted associates. He was one of the only other people who knew about my plans. PO shifted in the chair on the three chairs in front of my desk. The other two were vacant.

"You think that I should have told him sooner?"

PO shrugged his shoulders. "Julian, you know I would never tell you how to handle your business, but you know your son," he answered as he shook his head. "He's not going to like the fact that you brought Aaron up to run things. On top of that, he's definitely not going to like the fact that you've been planning this for the last three months without saying anything to him."

I nodded.

"True," I agreed. "But the way he's been carrying on the past few months is not representative of a levelheaded, thinking individual capable or mature enough to fill my shoes in my absence."

PO nodded. He was well aware of how Cameron's behavior. I sighed before I continued.

"He'll feel some type of way about it, but he doesn't have any other choice but to accept the new direction. At the end of the day, it's about taking care of business and our finances."

Before I could continue, my housekeeper Yolanda buzzed through the intercom letting me know that my guest had arrived.

"Send him up."

Moments later, there was a knock on the office door.

"Come in."

Aaron let himself into the room and closed the door. He greeted us before sitting down next to PO.

"What's up?" he asked casually.

"This won't take too long," I told him, "but you know I'm leaving for Cali on Wednesday. It's time to bring Cameron up to speed on our plans and how things are going to go for the next few months or so."

Aaron nodded. Up until that point, he had no idea that Cameron was still in the dark about our plans. Almost as if on cue, the door opened a few seconds later. Cameron made his way into the room.

"What's up y'all?"

"Speak of the devil," PO laughed.

Cameron laughed as well and made his way over to give me a hug. "What's up Pops?" he asked before taking the empty seat next to Aaron.

"I don't want to keep you from your weekend plans, so I'll just get right to it," I stated while continuing to stand in front of my desk. "Cameron, you know I'm leaving in a few days to check on your grandmother and her health condition. We need to go over the logistics of how things are going to run while I'm out of town."

I watched Cameron suspiciously cut his eyes towards Aaron. "You know we got you Pops," Cameron said, turning his attention back towards me. "Anything you need."

I nodded and walked around to my desk chair. "I'm glad that you feel that way, because Aaron is going to assist the operation in my absence."

Cameron frowned immediately. He cut his eyes at Aaron again before looking back at me. "What do you mean?"

"I mean that we've got a lot going on with the business right now. In the interest of protecting both the business and our finances I've put together a plan to take care of business while I'm out of town," I responded. "I think your grandmother is sicker than she's letting on. There's no telling how long I will be out there."

"You didn't think I can handle running everything by myself, so you went and got me a babysitter?" Cameron's tone was harsh.

My jaw tightened.

Aaron leaned forward in his seat and turned towards Cameron. "Aye, man, nobody is trying to undermine you. We all have a lot invested in this operation. We just thought –"

"Excuse me, but I was speaking to my father," Cameron snapped.

I quickly interjected. "Watch your tone, son."

"Nah it's cool, Julian," Aaron said, settling back into his chair.

"No, it's not," I said as I looked Cameron directly in the eyes. "Now I've spent the last thirty years building my reputation in business and in these streets. The Reid name would mean nothing around this city without the partnership and support of Aaron and his father. You need to show some respect."

Cameron didn't respond but maintained his eye contact with me.

"This plan has already been well thought out and prepared. I'm just bringing you up to speed. The three of you need to work together to make sure that things keep rolling along ... smoothly. Do you think you can handle that, Cameron?"

Cameron maintained his fierce eye contact with me for a few moments longer before he leaned back in his chair and answered, "Yeah."

"Good. Then let's get started."

BLUE

I cut my eyes over to my passenger seat while I continued to navigate my Dodge Charger towards my destination. I turned the music up a little louder to avoid any further conversation because I was not in the mood for any small talk. When it came to handling business, I was quick and efficient, and I normally preferred to work alone. I never liked working with anybody new. The only reason why I even had this kid Dre riding shotgun was because Cameron had personally vouched for him and insisted that I show him the ropes.

Ten minutes later, I parked on the street near our destination. I shut off the engine and grabbed my gun, tucking it securely in my waistband. I hopped out of the car and turned towards Dre.

"Don't speak unless you're spoken to."

Dre nodded and followed me to the front door of the house. I knocked twice, and a few moments later the door cracked open.

"Aye Blue, what's up?" the stone-faced young man asked, standing in the doorway.

"What's up, Trez?" I asked. "You gonna let me in or what?" Trez nodded towards Dre.

"Who the fuck is this?" he asked with a frown.

"Oh this is Dre," I introduced the two. "One of Cam's new men."

Trez glared at Dre but opened the door a little wider and hesitantly let us into the house.

"Aye, man, lighten up," I said as I playfully hit Trez in the chest after walking further inside.

Trez shrugged his shoulders. "H-Town is in the back, but your boy stays in the living room."

I laughed and shook my head.

"Alright, man. Whatever," I said. "Dre, cool it out here. I'll be back in a minute. Trez, keep an eye on my car."

Dre and Trez both nodded in agreement. Dre sat down on the sofa and started playing with his phone while Trez stood by the front window. I continued down the narrow hallway that led to a den in the rear of the house. I knocked on the cracked door twice before pushing it open. H-Town, who was one of the biggest dealers for the Reid family, was seated at what appeared to be a card table smoking a cigar as he counted money. After years of doing business with each other, we had developed a good friendship.

"C'mon H, you know I like to be in and out," I joked with him. "You were supposed to be finished counting the money before I got here."

"And your ass was supposed to be here like two hours ago," H-Town commented through a cloud of smoke.

I laughed and shrugged my shoulders. "My bad, man. I got a

little slowed down because Cam got me doing ride-a-longs with some new niggas."

H-Town shook his head. "You know I don't mess with no new niggas," he said, "but anyway, the money is over there in that bag. I'm just counting something for my baby mama."

"Which one?" I joked.

"Fuck you, nigga," H-Town laughed. "You know Tasha is the only one that stresses me for cash."

I picked up the black duffel bag that was sitting on the floor in a corner of the room. "Damn, this shit is heavy," I said, shouldering the bag.

H-Town smiled and said, "What can I say, man? Business is good."

"Don't I know it," I agreed. After a few more moments of small talk, I said, "Well, let me get this out of here. I need to finish these pickups, and then drop off the new boy. Hell, I'm trying to see my own baby mama before the end of the day."

"That's what's up man," H-Town said as we slapped hands.

I readjusted the bag on my shoulder. With one hand on the doorknob, I joked, "If business stays this good, I'm going to need a bigger trunk."

As soon as H-Town laughed, there was a loud noise in the front of the house that startled us both.

BOOM!

BOOM!

BOOM!

AARON

Still seated in front of his desk, I watched Julian stand in front of the large window to his office, staring down at the driveway. I heard Cameron slam his car door and speed off. Julian shook his head and sighed heavily. PO stood up, clearing his throat.

"Julian, I think I'm about to go on and head out too," he said. "I'll hit you up before you leave on Wednesday."

The two said their goodbyes and PO left Julian and I alone in the office.

"How do you think that went over?" Julian shook his head again and laughed.

I laughed and shrugged my shoulders. "I mean, I think it went as we all expected it would," I answered. "You already knew that he would feel some type of way about me being here. He was expecting to be in charge."

"Yeah, but it's not like he isn't used to answering to someone other than me. When Deuce was around, Cameron always took the backseat."

"I hear you," I said, "but Deuce isn't around anymore. It's obvious Cameron was expecting to have a bigger role now. He was expecting to be the one in the driver's seat while you're away."

"He hasn't shown me that he can take control of the wheel just yet," Julian responded evenly.

I nodded. Julian was right. From what I heard, Cameron was nowhere near ready to take control of his father's business.

"But he's going to come around," Julian stated. I gave him a look of skepticism, but Julian continued. "He will come around, Aaron. He loves his family and his money too much not to. Trust me on this."

I shrugged my shoulders again. "I guess we'll see."

Julian nodded. "Well, I'm going to let you go and get to the rest of your weekend," he said. "I'm sure you have some plans."

A smile tugged at my lips when I thought about Jada. "Actually, I do. I'm about to go meet up with my girl. Probably spend the rest of the weekend with her."

"Your girl, huh?" Julian questioned. "Looks like you've been enjoying your time in Atlanta a little bit more than I thought."

"Something like that," I answered. Changing the subject, I

asked, "Where's the rest of your family? I thought you would have a house full on a holiday weekend."

"Cameron doesn't necessarily want to be around me right now," Julian joked, "and my older daughter is out of town visiting her husband's family. I'm just going to chill and do a little more packing. Besides, we're all getting together for my younger daughter's birthday on Tuesday."

I sat up a little straighter in my seat.

"Oh yeah?"

"Yep. My baby girl is turning twenty-eight," Julian answered, "and Jada's had a really rough year, so I definitely didn't want to leave town before her birthday."

"Jada?"

I felt my cell phone vibrate in my pocket.

"Yeah. You remember my baby girl, don't you?" Julian questioned as he picked up a picture frame from his desk and handed it to me. "I know you haven't seen each other since you were little kids, but her mom and your mom grew up together. That's actually how I started doing business with your father."

I froze and stared at the picture of Jada in my hands. I was at a total loss for words. I knew something about her seemed familiar, but Julian was right. It had been many, many years since we last saw each other. Sure, our mothers had grown up together, but Jada and I were raised in two totally different states and never spent any real time around each other. I knew that Julian had kids, but I didn't remember their names. I did business with so many different people, it was hard to keep track of all the little details. Twenty-something years and a lot of curves later, Jada looked nothing like she did the last time we saw each other as young children.

I handed the picture back to Julian.

"That's the reason why I decided not to leave until Wednesday," Julian said, sitting the picture back down on his desk.

"Yeah," I nodded. "Let me go on and head out. I'll get with you before you leave town."

"That's cool," Julian said as he pulled his ringing cell phone out of his pocket. "Looks like I'm getting a call from Blue anyway."

We quickly said goodbye, and I exited his house. I slipped into the driver's seat of my Aston Martin and just sat behind the wheel for a minute. I grabbed my phone and looked to see a text from Jada asking where I was. If she only knew. I quickly responded and let her know I was on my way back to her. I sighed heavily before starting the engine to my car. I was going to have to find a way to tell Jada who I really was. Definitely before her birthday dinner on Tuesday.

JADA

"Oh, what's that smell?" I asked in a baby voice while I sat in the middle of the floor in Nisha's living room. "You made a stinky. Didn't you, little man?"

Vanessa and I were visiting our mutual friend, Nisha Sims. Nisha was the former longtime girlfriend turned fiancé of Kelvin Massey before he was killed the previous year. Vanessa and I grew up with Kelvin and his best friends, Israel Mann and Caleb Bridges. I was playing with Nisha's two-month-old son, Kyle, while he laid in his swing. Vanessa was stretched across the sofa texting her fiancé, Darius Jones – who we all referred to as DJ.

"Whew, Nisha! I hope you got some air freshener somewhere around here!" I shouted.

Vanessa laughed. "Yeah, girl. It smells like Kyle filled that diaper up!"

Nisha came out of the kitchen, wiping her hands on a dishtowel draped over her shoulder. She shook her head at us. "Y'all act like y'all are scared of a little baby poo," she joked. "Come here, little man."

Nisha bent down to pick Kyle up from his swing. She

grabbed his diaper bag and went to the loveseat, where she began to change his diaper. "Jada, I'm sorry I can't make it to your dinner tonight," she said to me, "but I'm really glad you stopped by. We've both been so busy these past few months. I feel like I've barely gotten to a chance to see you."

"Yeah, I know," I agreed. I stood up from the floor and sat next to Vanessa. "I've been so busy between the boutique, the restaurant, and trying to open this salon."

"And her new boyfriend," Vanessa added with a smile. "The boyfriend that we still haven't met."

"Oh yeah," Nisha said. "Ness told me that you have a new man. What's that all about?"

I blushed as a mile-wide smile spread across my face. "He is not the reason I've been ghost. I've just been really caught up with work."

"Mmm hmm," Nisha said unconvinced after she finished cleaning Kyle and placed him on her shoulder. "Where did y'all meet?"

"She met him at Shannon's birthday party a few months ago. You know the party that I had to bully her out of the house for," Vanessa explained.

"Ha! I remember that," Nisha laughed.

"Whatever," I rolled my eyes. "Yes. I met him at the party. We've pretty much been together ever since then. He's meeting my family tonight."

"Are you serious?" Nisha shouted. "You're bringing your new man around your crazy ass family?"

All three of us started to laugh.

"Y'all my family is not that bad!"

"Bullshit!" Vanessa laughed. "Girl, Ayanna is mean as hell, and intimidating doesn't even begin to describe Cameron and your dad. Julian used to scare the piss outta me when we were younger."

"And don't forget Aunt Vita," Nisha said, as she continued to rock Kyle on her shoulder.

I sighed as I hung my head. "Oh, Aunt Vita."

"Exactly!" Vanessa laughed even harder. "Once she gets a couple of glasses of wine in her system you never know what's going to come out of her mouth."

I frowned. "You're right. Damn … I'm actually kind of nervous now," I said. "I'm not sure he knows what he's walking into."

"We're just messing with you girl. He will be okay," Nisha attempted to reassure me.

"Yeah, Jay. If he's already met Ayanna and survived that, the rest of the family should be a piece of cake," Vanessa added.

"Hell yeah," Nisha agreed. "I didn't know he had already met Ayanna. If he's survived that, you don't have anything to be worried about."

I laughed and looked down at my watch. I needed to drop Vanessa off at her place before I headed home to start getting ready for dinner. "Well, I need to get home and change, but I'm sure that Ness will give you a play by play tomorrow," I told Nisha.

"You're damn right!" Vanessa laughed, standing up from the couch.

Nisha laughed and hugged us both. "I can't wait to hear all about it," she said. "Enjoy, Jada … and happy birthday again."

AARON

Luke inhaled deeply on the blunt before he passed it back to me. Before he could open his mouth to speak, my ringing cell phone disturbed the silence between us. Luke shook his head when he saw Jada's name appear on the screen. I exhaled deeply before answering the phone.

"Hey mama," I said with my phone in one hand and the blunt in the other.

"Hey where are you?" she asked. "Are you headed this way?"

I looked down at my watch and sighed again. I was supposed to pick her up so we could ride to her birthday dinner together. However, I was still at my house and not quite finished meeting with Luke. "Damn, babe. Look, don't get mad, but I had something work-related come up. I'm running a little behind schedule," I told her. "Can I meet you there?"

Jada paused for a moment. "Yeah. Sure," she answered. I could tell that she was trying to hide her disappointment. "How late do you think you might be?"

I looked down at my watch again.

"I'll be there before nine. I promise."

"Okay. I'll see you then."

She ended the call. I dropped the phone back down by my side and looked up at Luke.

"Nigga ... you still ain't told her?"

I shook my head and passed the blunt back to him. "Nah."

"Black, what the fuck?" he asked, shaking his head in disbelief. "You just gonna walk your happy ass in the restaurant like 'Hey Julian, forgot to tell you I've been fucking your daughter. Oh, and hey, babe; your daddy's on my payroll'? Come on, man. You already know that's gonna go left."

I waved him off. "Ain't shit I can do about it now. It is what it is," I answered. "I'm just here to make money and handle business. We'll see how everything else plays out."

Luke shook his head. "Yeah right. Tell me anything, man. I've seen y'all together. Jada ain't just whatever to you. You actually care about her."

I shrugged my shoulders, desperate to change the subject. "Whatever, man. I didn't ask you over here to talk about that," I said. "I need to talk to you about this other shit with the Atlanta team. That's the main thing we need to be worried about."

"Speak on it then."

I spent the next half an hour filling Luke in on the plans to temporarily run the Atlanta market in Julian's absence. For the most part, I decided that business would continue to run as usual. Cameron would continue his same responsibilities – as well as Julian's other key players such as PO, Blue, Zo, etc. However, with Julian not being around I maintained full authority to make changes as I saw fit. Luke would be my right-hand man.

Since my arrival in Atlanta, things moved smoothly until the past weekend. After I left my meeting with Julian, PO, and Cameron, I received word that there were shootings and disturbances at a number of our stash houses. There was no explanation behind it, but I found the timing to be suspicious. I had to get to the bottom of things soon. My plan over the next few weeks would be to familiarize Luke with the day to day operations of Atlanta so that he could easily be my second set of eyes.

When Luke and I wrapped up our conversation, I walked him to the front door. He paused and glanced at his watch. "Guess you gotta head out, huh?" he asked me.

"Yeah, man," I answered with a nod.

Already dressed for the dinner, I just hoped I didn't run into any traffic on the way to the restaurant.

"Well, good luck, my nigga. Let me know how that shit goes," Luke said before he headed towards his car.

I closed the door behind Luke and sighed heavily. I felt the beginning of a migraine. I honestly had no idea how things were going to play out at the restaurant. When I started dating Jada, I was just looking to have some fun. I knew that I was only in Atlanta temporarily, and I had not had any interest in a serious relationship in years. Between the business and raising my ten-year-old daughter, Olivia, I had not prioritized relationships in the least. To be honest, the last serious relationship I had was with Olivia's mother, Isabela.

Somehow, over the course of the last few months, I started to picture a future with Jada. However, after discovering that she was Julian Reid's daughter, I started to wonder how much we really knew about each other. Sure, I had not been completely honest with my occupation and where my permanent residence was. I did tell her the truth about my family structure, but I had withheld my parents' names. Jada knew that I was the middle child with an older and a younger sister. She knew all about Olivia and that Olivia's mother was no longer in the picture. I also shared with her that Olivia was living with my parents in Miami.

Although Jada shared details with me about her past relationships, she was a little vague when it came to sharing information about her family. I realized that if she was more forthcoming, I would have connected the dots sooner. Even armed with the revelation that Jada was Julian Reid's daughter, I didn't want things to end. There was much more to her than her slick mouth and curvy physique that initially caught my attention. She was incredibly independent and had a lot going for herself in regard to her career. She ran a successful family restaurant, a clothing boutique, and was preparing to open a salon with her sister. Knowing who her father was, I knew that we were raised in similar lifestyles. In my eyes that made us even more compatible. She was built for the life that I lived. Jada was the complete opposite of Olivia's mother.

I made my way to the garage and slid into the passenger seat of my Maserati. I knew that Jada would have every right to be upset with me when she found out the truth. I just hoped that she would be willing to hear me out.

JADA

My guests and I were seated in a private dining room at The Capital Grille restaurant. We had already received our drinks and would soon be placing our meal orders. I looked down at my cell phone and saw it was ten minutes until nine. I shook my head in disappointment before my aunt's voice broke into my thoughts.

"So, who is he, baby?" Aunt Vita questioned as she raised her glass to her lips and took a sip of her wine.

I looked up from my cell phone. "What?"

"Who is he?" Aunt Vita repeated her question. "The man that we're waiting on. Who is supposed to be sitting next to you?"

A hush fell over the table. No one besides Vita was looking directly at me, but I knew that they were all waiting to hear my response. I realized that I had spent the last few months so preoccupied with Aaron and work that I had neglected to inform my family that I was even dating someone new. Ayanna and Vanessa were the only ones at the table that knew he existed.

I shrugged my shoulders before casually answering, "The guy I've been seeing."

I raised my own glass of wine and took a long sip.

"Well would you look at that," Aunt Vita said with a big grin. "You got yourself a new boyfriend already?"

"Already?"

"Yeah, baby. Israel's barely back in Texas, and you done went and got yourself a new man," Aunt Vita commented. "I ain't mad at that. I just never thought we would see the end of that drama with Israel."

This time, the table was completely silent as eyes darted back and forth between my aunt and me. My eyes were narrowed, and my jaw was clenched while I glared at Vita. However, my aunt was oblivious to my stare and continued to sip her drink. The waitress came back into the room to check on our party, and Vita ordered another drink. Once the waitress left, I spoke again.

"Auntie, he's moved on with his life and so have I. I am *very* happy with my current relationship and would prefer if we didn't discuss Israel any further," I stated.

Vita raised her hands defensively and sat back in her seat. My dad cut his eyes towards his baby sister and shook his head in a disapproving manner. Slowly but surely the side conversations resumed. Not wanting to engage in any conversation, I sat in my seat quietly. A few moments later my cell phone started to vibrate. A smile spread across my face when I saw Aaron's name.

"Hey are you here?"

"Yeah. Come meet me out front right quick," he said quickly.

"What?" I asked. "Babe, we're all waiting for you. Come inside. The hostess can show you to the room."

"Jada, for real," he said. "Come out front for a moment."

"Fine," I said, hesitantly standing up from the table.

I excused myself from the room and quickly made my way outside where Aaron was waiting. He looked amazing in the tailored black suit and a slim fit black button-down with the top two buttons undone. I could not wait until I could take it off of him later that night. I walked up to him placing both hands on the sides of his face and kissing his lips.

"I'm glad you finally made it," I said. "Come on."

I turned on my heels to head back into the restaurant, but Aaron grabbed my hand and pulled me back towards him.

"Jada, we need to talk real quick."

I frowned at him. "Baby, there will be plenty of time to talk later," I whined. "I'm hungry."

I turned around again. Aaron held onto my hand, but I pulled him along with me. When we stepped into the private dining room, all eyes were on us. I noticed that my brother and father exchanged looks of confusion. I held Aaron's hand tighter and led him to our chairs. Once we were seated, I noticed smiles and nods of approval from the women at the table. Out of the corner of my eye, I noticed my father's stone-faced expression.

Cameron, who sat directly across from Aaron, had eyes full of malice while he glared at him.

Vanessa cleared her throat. "Jada ... would you like to introduce us all to your boyfriend?"

I smiled but was interrupted before I could speak.

"Boyfriend?" my father asked in confusion.

"Aaron, what the fuck is going on?" Cameron questioned.

My eyes widened at my brother. I turned my attention towards my dad and asked, "You know him?"

My father sighed but didn't respond. I turned to look at Aaron with my angry glare fixed on him.

"How do you know my father?"

Aaron leaned closer to me. Under the table, he placed a hand on top of mine, but I pulled away from him.

"Answer me, dammit."

Aaron's voice was low, and he tried to speak in a hushed tone. "That's why I called you outside. I was trying to find a way to tell you," he said. "Baby, I –"

"Baby?" Cameron interrupted.

"Cameron!" I shot an angry glare towards my brother.

My eyes quickly darted around the dinner table. Everyone avoided eye contact with me. Cameron was still glaring at Aaron and my dad was shaking his head while looking down at the table. Aaron was the only one looking at me, and he rubbed my thigh in an attempt to calm me. Everyone else was either whispering to the person next to them, on their cellphones, or sipping their drinks.

"Daddy," I said. "How do you know him?"

My father hesitated but then looked at me directly and answered my question. "He's Manny Mercer's son."

I took in a sharp breath. I felt as if the air was sucked from my lungs. Several people in the room knew who Manny Mercer was. I shook my head and tried to blink back the tears that were starting to form in my eyes. I removed Aaron's hand from my thigh and pushed my chair away from the table. I stood up, grabbing my cellphone and purse.

"I've got to get out of here," I mumbled.

Vanessa stood up and started to move towards me, but Aaron motioned for her to stop. He spoke to my father while I headed for the door.

"Julian, I'm sorry. I'll give you a call later."

Aaron stood up from the table and started to follow me. I practically ran outside of the restaurant but had to wait for the valet to bring my car around. Aaron caught up with me while I stood on the curb.

"Jada!"

I glanced over my shoulder and rolled my eyes at him. "You lied to me."

"Yes. I did," he said. "I lied about what I do for a living, but Jada … I didn't know you were Julian's daughter until Saturday."

"Then you should have told me then," I stated firmly, turning around to face him. I was careful not to raise my voice as there were other restaurant patrons waiting for valet as well. "I've been in your home and in your bed every night since then. You had plenty of opportunities to tell me who you really were before we were sitting in a room full of my closest family and friends."

Aaron sighed heavily and took a step closer to me. He placed a hand on my hip and pulled my body towards his. I did not resist.

"You're right. I should have told you," he agreed. "There's no excuse for that, and I am truly sorry. Jada, regardless of who our parents are, the way we feel about each other is real. There's no denying this thing between us."

I shook my head. "This wasn't a little white lie that can easily be swept under the rug. My last relationship was ruined because of the business connections that he and his friends had with my father. You are literally my dad's connect. Aaron, this is major."

I pulled away from him and angrily wiped away a tear that had fallen onto my cheek.

"I hear you, but we can work this out," he said. "Can we at least go somewhere and talk?"

I could see the remorse written all over his face. I was torn between my heart and my mind. However, before I could answer him the valet attendant returned with my car and my keys. I broke my eye contact with Aaron and reached into my purse for some cash. I handed the attendant a ten-dollar bill and hopped into my car. I sped off before Aaron could say anything else.

CAMERON

I was right behind Shannon when she unlocked the front door to our home. In an attempt to strengthen our relationship, I had asked her to move in a few months earlier. Unfortunately, we had problems ever since. Shannon entered the house silently and disarmed the alarm system. She set her purse and keys on the table in the foyer. I immediately started to unbutton my shirt after pulling it out of my slacks. I followed Shannon into the kitchen where she poured herself a glass of wine.

"That shit is fucking crazy. That nigga has been fucking my sister for months and didn't have the decency to say something to my dad," I commented. "Nigga, didn't even tell her who the hell he was."

Shannon took a long sip of her wine before looking at me. "Jada is grown, Cameron. She can take care of herself," she said. "I don't want to spend my evening talking about other people and their relationship issues."

I shook my head in frustration. Things between us had been strained for a number of months. It started before my disappearance on the night of her birthday, but things had not gotten any better as time passed. I actually hadn't even been sleeping at our house for the past week. I hoped that the family dinner would be a step in the right direction for us, but things had not gone as planned for any of the parties involved.

Without another word, Shannon left the kitchen and started towards the staircase. I was close on her heels.

"Hey ... wait a minute," I said, catching up to her.

Halfway up the stairs, Shannon stopped and turned to face me.

"You going to bed? I was hoping that we could at least talk for a minute or something," I told her.

"Cam, I agreed to go to the dinner tonight because I like your sister. I actually like your whole family," she said, "but things are not cool between me and you. You haven't been here in nearly a week. I don't feel like talking. It's late, and I have to work in the morning. Why don't you just go back to wherever you've been laying your head this week?"

I stood quietly and watched Shannon disappear up the stairs. I didn't know how things had gone so wrong between us. Before her, I never considered myself to be a one-woman man, but Shannon was special to me. I occasionally messed around with other women from time to time, but she was the only one that had my heart. Throughout our relationship the other women I dealt with on the side had come and gone, none of them lingering around for more than a few weeks or so. Somehow my situation with Brianna had taken a hold of me. I knew that she was partly responsible for the growing distance between Shannon and me. Although Shannon was suspicious, I was certain she did not specifically know about Brianna, and there was no way I was going to tell her. I knew that Shannon would leave me for good if she ever knew the details of my situation with Brianna.

I hesitated at the bottom of the stairs. I knew that leaving would only set us back even further. However, there was a lot on my mind at the moment – including the revelation of Aaron and Jada's relationship and the hand that Aaron would directly be playing in my family's business for the weeks or months to come. I didn't want to add any further stress. I knew that if I went up the stairs to confront Shannon, I would only have more frustration to deal with. So instead, I turned around and grabbed my keys. Moments later, I was in my car and heading where I knew I could clear my mind and not have to think about my troubles until the morning. I started the engine to my Challenger. It was a short drive to my destination.

"Hey, you," Brianna said sweetly when she greeted me at her front door. She kissed me on the lips and stepped to the side so I could enter her apartment. She looked down at her watch. "I didn't think I would get to see you tonight. I thought you said you had a family thing."

"I did, but that wrapped up a whole lot quicker than I thought it would," I said, sitting down on her living room sofa.

"Is everything okay?" she asked.

I shrugged my shoulders, and Brianna joined me on the couch. "It's not anything I want to talk about," I said while I pulled her onto my lap.

"We don't have to talk at all if you don't want," Brianna said as she wrapped her arms around my neck and kissed my lips.

JULIAN

I let out a deep sigh and tried to digest the information Blue shared with me. I ran my hands over my face and sat down on the edge of my desk. Bluehad just informed me of another robbery at one of our main stash houses. I was irritated to say the least.

"Who was supposed to be on lookout?" I asked.

"JB, but he wasn't there when it happened."

"What do you mean?" I asked with a frown.

"He had left to grab something to eat. Apparently one of the new boys was there," he answered.

"And that doesn't sound suspicious to you?"

Blue shrugged his shoulders. "We're looking at everything from all angles right now trying to connect the dots," he told me. "I know you're getting ready to head out of town, but I just thought you might want to know. I'm sure Lil' Mercer is going to get to the bottom of everything."

"Yeah. He's supposed to be stopping by here shortly," I said. "We have a number of things to discuss."

I didn't share the events of the previous night with him. I figured if Aaron and Jada continued their relationship then Blue and everyone else would find out soon enough. In my absence, both Blue and PO would be working closely with Aaron. A knock on the door interrupted us. Assuming that it was Aaron, I told the person to come in. Blue and I both looked towards the door to see Jada entering the room.

She did not look happy.

"Alright, Julian. That's my cue," Blue said. "Take it easy, man. I hope everything is straight with your mom."

I nodded and Blue excused himself from the room, closing the door behind him. I glanced at the time on my watch. Aaron was set to arrive at any minute.

"Jada, it's not really a good time. I –"

"You're leaving in a matter of hours, Dad," she cut me off. "There won't be another time."

She walked further into the room and sat down in the chair that Blue occupied moments earlier. I released a tired sigh.

"What's on your mind?"

"How long is he going to be here?"

"I won't know the answer to that question until I get out there and see what's really going on with your grandmother," I answered. "It could be a few months or more."

My response was less detailed than Jada would have liked,

but it was honest. I had no idea how long I would be out of town. Jada shook her head in frustration.

"I won't really have an accurate idea of your grandmother's medical condition until I get there. There are a lot of things going on with the business, and it's probably not an ideal time for me to be away. That's why Aaron's here. I need to be with your grandmother, and Aaron and his father are the only two people I fully trust to ensure that things run as smooth as possible," I said. I paused for a moment. "Jada, how did you even meet him?"

"I met him at a club a few months ago," she answered softly. "The night we all went out for Shannon's birthday."

"So, this has been going on for over three months?" I asked.

Jada nodded. "Yeah, but it's over now. So, there's nothing for you to be worried about."

"Jada, I'm not worried about that. I'm worried about you," I told her. "I don't know how you keep ending up in situations with people I'm involved with."

"Dad, do you think I enjoy this shit?" Jada asked. "The past year was hell for me, but I thought that I was past all that. I thought that I was in a place to let go of Israel and all the drama that came along with him. A lot of drama that stemmed from his involvement with people who were connected to you. The last thing I wanted to do was end up in bed with another one of your business associates."

I nodded. "I hear what you're saying, baby girl, but Aaron isn't just another one of my business associates."

"Dad, I am quite aware of your connection to his family."

I shook my head. "No. What I'm saying is that I've been working with him and his father for a long time. I've seen him grow and mature into a powerful, responsible, levelheaded man," I explained. "He is totally different from Israel and his friends. Aaron would keep you far removed from his business and make sure that you are protected. What I'm saying is that it wouldn't be the worst thing in the world if you chose to continue your relationship with him."

"You have got to be kidding me," Jada said in disbelief. "Dad, he lied to me for months. He told me he worked in marketing or some shit. He said he didn't know who I was until this past weekend but prior to that he completely misled me on who he is."

"Did you tell him about me?"

"What?"

"Look Jada ... I'm not saying that he was right for lying to you. I'm not saying that at all, but I'm surprised you don't understand why he doesn't walk around announcing who he is to any and everybody," I said. "If you had been a little more upfront with your family information, he would have known who you were a whole lot sooner. You both had your own reasons for withholding information."

Jada hopped up from her chair and grabbed her purse. "Have a safe flight, Dad," she said as she hugged me and kissed me on the cheek. "Tell Nana I love her."

"Baby girl, you can't keep running from things and expect to resolve anything," I told her.

Jada nodded but didn't respond as she continued towards the office door. When she opened it, Aaron was standing there with his fist raised as if he were about to knock. Jada froze in the doorway. Aaron's hand dropped and his shoulders relaxed while he slid his hands into his pants pockets.

"I tried to call you several times last night," he said to her.

"Yeah, and I ignored you several times last night," Jada responded harshly.

"Jada, look I –"

"We're not about to do this right now," she interrupted him. "Talk to my dad. That's the reason you're here, right?"

Aaron sighed in response. Jada pushed past him and left. Aaron walked into the room and closed the door.

"When are you headed out?" he asked.

"Soon. My flight leaves in couple of hours," I responded. I stood up from the edge of the desk and walked behind it. I started to pack some papers into a briefcase. "Blue just left a little bit ago."

"Cool. So, I guess he already brought you up to speed on the stash house situation?" Aaron asked.

I nodded.

"I got my man Luke on it. He and PO are securing another location, and I'mma holla at the young boys out there tomorrow," Aaron said. "What do you know about these kids Dre and Carlos?"

"They've been around for a few months. Cameron vetted them," I answered. "He put them on with some of the street crew. Why?"

Aaron shrugged his shoulders. "I don't know, but something's not right," he replied. "I just want to make sure that I'm not missing anything.

"I know you'll figure it out," I told him. "I have no worries about leaving things in your hands."

"There's no need for you to worry at all. I know you're probably feeling like now isn't a good time for you to be leaving, but you need to take care of your mom, man," Aaron said. "Everybody understands that."

"Checking on her is definitely my main priority right now, but you know ... I'm still deciding if I'm going to step away from things permanently."

Aaron waved me off. "We don't even have to talk about that right now," he said. "We'll see how everything plays out."

There was a moment of silence between us while I continued to pack by briefcase.

"You know ... I really didn't know that she was your daughter until you showed me that picture on Saturday," Aaron's voice broke the silence in the room.

I stopped packing and looked up at him.

"Jada's a lot to handle. Just make sure you look after her, okay? She will never admit that she needs protection, but she does. Cameron can take care of himself. Ayanna has Tony, but Jada ... she's the only one that I still worry about, especially with everything that's gone on the last year or so."

"You don't have to worry about that, Julian. I'll keep an eye on her for sure," Aaron said. "I care about your daughter."

I nodded in agreement and zipped up my bag. "Good," I said. I made my way to the other side of the desk and patted Aaron on the shoulder. "Why don't you help me carry my bags downstairs?"

MICHAELA

I took a sip of my sweet tea and then settled into my chair. I looked around the crowded BBQ restaurant and rolled my eyes in disgust before looking at my twin brother, Mikey. I hated BBQ, and I hated Atlanta. However, we had a job to do – a job that I was taking very seriously even if my brother wasn't.

"Are you done?"

"Almost. Damn! What's the rush?" Mikey asked between bites of his pulled pork sandwich. "We're not getting up with them boys for another hour or so."

"It's not that, Mike," I responded, visibly annoyed. "You know that I hate being in crowded places like this."

Mikey sat his sandwich down and grabbed a napkin to wipe his hands. "Relax," he said. "People may have heard of us, but how many people in Atlanta have seen our faces? Not many. Most of the people who see our faces don't live to tell about it."

Mikey laughed and took a sip of his drink. I rolled my eyes and ran my fingers through my hair. My lengthy tresses were curled to perfection and the manicure on my nails was fresh. I was dressed in designer clothes from head to toe and sported a flawless full face of makeup. No one would have ever suspected that I was one of the deadliest contract killers on the East coast.

I looked back at my brother and rolled my eyes again. I loved him, but it was obvious that I was the more serious sibling. Our names were Mikey and Michael Pitt. However, we were known as the Hit Twins – the deadly duo that made a living via murder for hire for the better part of a decade. We started our careers under the wing of a well-known contract killer, but after his retirement, we went into business for ourselves. We were hired by several criminal organizations to eliminate their competitors and their enemies. The statement Mikey made was accurate. Almost all of our marks were successfully eliminated. It was well known across many state lines that if the Hit Twins were after you, you were as good as gone. Based out of the DMV area, we did not make too many visits to the South. That was why Mikey felt more at ease than I did. He was almost sure no one would know us there.

Although my brother made a valid point, I was normally the more levelheaded twin. I was hesitant to throw caution to the wind. I did not expect our next job to be easy, but that's why we were always prepared. It would take patience and strategy to get to our target, but I was prepared to do whatever I needed to do in order to make sure that we achieved success.

LUKE

THREE WEEKS LATER

I spotted PO and Blue when I stepped into the restaurant even though their backs were towards me. As I approached the table, I paused a few feet away before making my presence known. I overheard part of their conversation.

PO shook his head before taking a sip from his glass of water. "So where is the young boy now?" he asked.

Blue shrugged his shoulders. "I don't know man. After Aaron spoke to him a couple of weeks ago, Cam put him on something else," he answered. "He said he didn't want Aaron questioning his people."

"Don't that nigga realize that we're all the same people?" PO shook his head in disbelief.

"I know, man. Julian ain't been gone a whole month yet, and Cameron's jealousy is already starting to influence his decisions," Blue responded. "Things ain't been rolling smooth for a minute. You know that shit ain't gonna fly with the Mercers."

"I know. I'm surprised Aaron has been chill about everything so far," PO said. "I'd be surprised if that shit lasts much longer."

"Don't worry. It won't," I said as I walked up to the table.

I laughed as I greeted the pair.

"Look at you two sitting over here gossiping like a bunch of bitches," I joked.

Over the past couple of weeks, we had built a friendly working rapport.

"Fuck outta here," Blue waved me off as I slid into a chair to join them at the table.

PO shook his head and he scooted his chair closer to the table. "We were just talking about your boss and our boss's son."

"I figured," I said, shaking my head. "Like I said though, Aaron ain't gonna have too much more patience with your boy. If shit keeps going sideways, Aaron's gonna have to get things in line before Manny makes his way up here. Trust me, y'all don't want that shit to happen."

PO and Blue nodded in agreement. Throughout their years of working at Julian's side, they had come in contact with Manny Mercer less than a handful of times. Still, everyone knew how Manny operated. There would be nothing smooth about his approach if he had to be the one to get Atlanta under control.

"So, what's up, man?" Blue asked. "Why'd you call us out here today?"

"We have a new spot," I told them. "We're not going to be doing meetups at any of Julian's usual locations while he's gone. Cameron and his girl ain't cool right now so we're not going to be posted up at his place either. I'll text you the address when we leave. I've got five keys – one for each of you, me, Cameron, and Aaron. Nobody needs to go in or out without one of us being there, especially until we figure out what's going on."

"That makes sense," PO agreed.

"Something isn't sitting right," I said. "As often as things move around, there have been too many robberies and shit taking place. There are too many in the crew getting jacked for cash or product when we aren't very vocal about the moves that we make. We always switch up the routine. It's like someone has inside information with the way the enemy is always two steps ahead. Shit ain't adding up. It's too similar to the problems y'all had with KS9."

"Sounds like you're convinced that someone on our team is dirty," PO stated.

I shrugged my shoulders. "That is yet to be determined, but it looks that way. We're gonna get to the bottom of it though. Trust that," I said. "I don't know about y'all, but I damn sure don't want Manny Mercer coming up here."

I picked up the menu and looked it over.

"What's good here?" I asked.

AARON

I was starting to wonder what I had gotten myself into by volunteering to come to Atlanta. Nothing had been going right, and I almost wondered if I should have just stayed in Miami and let my dad handle it. After almost a month, things were getting worse with Julian's team and tension between Cameron and me was steadily rising. I was missing out on time with my daughter while the Atlanta operation was facing some of the same issues they battled with KS9. The only thing that had gone right was the time I spent with Jada before she found out the truth, but we had barely spoken in weeks. I was almost tired of trying to get through to her.

I pulled the blunt away from my lips and released a thick cloud of smoke. I stepped out that night to distract myself from everything that was going on. I really just wanted to be alone, but I knew better than to go out to a club by myself. Instead, I was with Luke and a few of our men. I thought the strip club would have been the perfect setting to distract me from my problems, but the alcohol, weed, and naked women actually did nothing to ease my mind. One of my goons approached me and interrupted my thoughts.

"Aye, boss, there's some chick trying to see you," he informed me.

"What's her name?" I asked over the loud music.

"Kara Ross."

I sighed heavily. I should have just stayed my ass at home.

Sensing my irritation, he said, "I can tell her to get lost if you want me to."

I shook my head. "It's cool. Let her through," I said. "She ain't gonna leave quietly, and I ain't trying to deal with her tantrums tonight."

He disappeared and moments later Kara was standing in front of me. As usual, she looked appealing to the eye. The dress she wore left very little to the imagination and ordinarily would have had my dick standing at attention. However, all I could think about was Jada. I tried to call her a few times earlier in the evening. Each time she sent me to voicemail. Instead, we traded a few text messages back and forth.

Kara winked at me before sitting at the table and cozying up to me.

"I'm surprised to see you out tonight," she said. "Every time I've tried to reach you you've been busy."

"I've had a lot of shit going on."

"All work and no play makes Aaron a dull boy," she said, reaching under the table to rub my thigh.

I didn't respond. Instead, I raised the blunt to my lips again.

"The way you've been dodging me I thought you found another girl or something, but I see you're here by yourself tonight," she said. She moved her hand up my leg, eventually stroking my crotch. She leaned in closer to me and whispered in my ear, "You know you don't have to leave here alone tonight, and you didn't have to come to a strip club to see a naked woman lift her legs up to her ears."

My shoulders dropped, and I shook my head as I tried to fight the smirk that was coming to my face. Kara was definitely entertaining between the sheets, but she didn't really hold my attention outside of the bedroom anymore. I pulled her hand away.

"I'll keep that in mind," I said as I stood up. "I gotta run to the men's room."

As I started to walk away, I felt my phone vibrate in my pocket. Jada responded to one of my many text messages. I was surprised she was still awake at that time of night. Her message said that she wasn't over it, and she didn't want to talk. That shit frustrated me even further. It had been over three weeks. How much more time did she need?

After using the bathroom, I was ready to go. I didn't mind hanging with my guys, but I wanted to leave the club. I found Luke and suggested we take the party back to my house, and he started to gather the crew. I hesitated before I made my way back over to Kara. For a brief moment, I considered taking her back to my place and giving her what she wanted, but I knew I would regret that shit when I woke up. When I approached her, I didn't bother sitting down at the table.

"It was good seeing you tonight, but I'm about to dip."

"Let me guess," she said as she stood up and placed her hands on her hips. "You've got an early start in the morning?"

I shrugged my shoulders.

"That's fine, Aaron," she said. "One day you're going to regret passing up on all of this."

I seriously doubted that.

"Maybe," I said. "Look, I'll hit you up sometime."

Kara laughed. "I've heard that before," she said. She kissed me on the cheek. "Enjoy the rest of your night."

I stood by the table watching her as she walked away. I prayed the day never came that I regretted moving on from her.

Moments later, Luke signaled me from the front door. I was ready to get out of there.

JADA

I rolled my eyes and turned on my side in my King-sized bed. I stared out of the windows in my bedroom, admiring my view of the city skyline. Despite the beauty of the city lights before me, I was beyond frustrated. I sighed heavily. There were a number of things that were bothering me, but I was mostly irritated by the fact that Aaron had been blowing up my phone all night. I tossed and turned in my bed unsuccessfully trying to go to sleep for the past three hours.

I repositioned my pillows under my head and shut my eyes in another attempt to doze off. Moments later, the peace and quiet of my condo was disturbed by the loud buzzing notification of my cell phone receiving yet another text message. I snatched the phone up and opened Aaron's message.

"I guess we've both said what we need to say. I know I was wrong, but I'm done trying to apologize to you. If this ain't what you want, then fine. It's not like I can't find your replacement tomorrow."

"*Excuse me!*" I shouted after reading his message out loud.

Who the hell was he talking to?

Angry, I sat up straight in my bed. I started to respond to his message but stopped myself. Instead, I called him. The phone rang until it eventually went to voicemail. I ended the call but immediately dialed his number again. It went straight to voicemail, and I hung up.

I was livid.

I looked over at my alarm clock and saw that it was a little after three o'clock in the morning. Pushing the covers back on my bed, I hopped to my feet. In less than five minutes, I got myself together to leave my place. I shed my night gown and dressed in a simple white T-shirt and a pair of gray leggings. I pulled my hair into a messy bun on top of my head. I paused for a moment to question my actions, but my anger had gotten the best of me.

I grabbed my phone and keys. After sliding my feet into a pair of Gucci slides, I headed for my car. Before I knew it, I pulled up to the security box at the gated entrance to Aaron's neighborhood.

"Ms. Reid, so nice to see you." I was greeted by Jerry, one of the security guards. "I'm surprised you weren't with Mr. Mercer. He just arrived a moment ago."

"I didn't really feel like partying tonight. I told him that I would meet up with him afterwards," I lied.

Jerry paused but maintained the smile on his face. "I see," he stated. "So, Mr. Mercer is expecting you?"

"He is."

"You know the drill though. Let me just call him really quick and let him know that you are here," Jerry said as he reached for the phone.

"You can try to reach him, but his phone is probably dead. His battery was low when I spoke to him earlier," I responded quickly. "It's probably just going to go to voicemail."

Jerry nodded in acknowledgment but continued to dial Aaron's number anyway. I smiled nervously and silently prayed that Aaron's phone was indeed dead or turned off. It was just my luck that the call went straight to voicemail.

"Straight to voicemail just like you said," Jerry said placing the phone back down on the receiver. "I'm just doing my job, Ms. Reid."

I nodded and smiled. "I know."

Jerry pushed the button to open the gate. "But don't let me find out that you two have broken up and you've turned into one of those crazy stalkers."

I laughed and pulled my truck towards the gate. "Have a good night Jerry!"

I navigated my way through the neighborhood until I pulled into Aaron's driveway. There were a couple of cars out front, but I parked next to his friend Luke's Tahoe. I jumped out of my Benz and stormed towards the front door. I could hear laughter and loud talking on the other side of the door. I knocked loudly.

There was no answer to my knocks.

Getting angrier by the second, I rang the doorbell three times and started to knock again. Some noise from inside the house quieted, and I heard heavy footsteps approaching the front door.

"Oh shit," I heard Luke say. "Aye, man, your girl is here."

I pressed my ear against the door. The conversation taking place was muffled, and I couldn't quite hear what Aaron had said.

"Luke! Open the goddamn door!" I shouted as I pounded on the door again.

Seconds later, the door swung open and I was standing face to face with Aaron.

"What the fuck are you doing beating on my damn door like you're crazy?" he barked.

I pushed past him and stepped into the foyer. I could see a group of people gathered in his great room with all eyes on me. I frowned at the group – some of them were familiar but most of them were not. There were several men in the group, but there was a number of women as well. Luke slowly backed out of the foyer and joined the crew of people gathered in the great room.

"Apparently I'm breaking up your little party," I said. "That's what the fuck I'm doing."

Aaron closed his eyes and shook his head. He pinched the bridge of his nose and let out a deep sigh.

"But the real question is what are you doing? Holding auditions for my replacement?" I questioned with more attitude while I motioned towards the women who were all dressed in revealing clothes.

Before Aaron could respond, Luke hopped up from the sofa and gathered the group. "Come on y'all. Let's take this somewhere else."

"Nah, man. You don't have to leave," Aaron said as the group started to pass him and head out the door.

Luke shook his head and placed a hand on Aaron's shoulder. "Bro, you got a situation on your hands that clearly needs some handling. I'll talk to you later." He turned towards me. "For the record Jada … the girls were with me."

I rolled my eyes in response. "Bye Luke."

Luke shrugged his shoulders and closed the door on his way out. Aaron and I stood in silence for a few moments with his menacing glare fixed on me. After a few more moments of uncomfortable silence, Aaron broke our eye contact and moved towards the front door. He locked it and set the alarm. I let out a quiet sigh of relief as I dropped my hands from where they had been resting on my hips. By locking the door and setting the alarm, Aaron let me know that he wasn't throwing me out of his house – not at that moment anyway.

Aaron brushed by me in silence and headed towards the kitchen. I hesitated for a moment but followed him. When I entered the kitchen, I saw that Aaron had poured a glass of wine for me and was opening a bottle of beer for himself. I slid onto one of the stools at the kitchen island and took a sip from my glass. Aaron stood on the other side of the kitchen island – drinking his beer and staring at me in silence.

"What do you want?" he eventually asked.

I frowned in response but didn't answer.

"Come on, Jada. It's late, and I'm tired," Aaron said. "What do you want?"

I took a sip of my wine and mumbled, "You didn't seem that tired a minute ago."

Aaron shook his head and let out a deep breath. He shoved his hands into the pockets of his pants and hesitated before he spoke again.

"Look," he said, "Something made you hop in that pretty little truck of yours and drive your ass over here at three o'clock in the morning. So, you can either speak up and say what's on your mind or you can sit down here and finish your glass alone while I go to bed."

"I didn't appreciate your tone earlier," I said as I stared down at my half-empty wine glass.

Aaron smirked. "You haven't answered the phone for me in weeks, but you somehow picked up on a tone through a text message?"

I looked up into his face.

"You know what I mean, Aaron."

"What did I say that bothered you?" he asked.

"It wasn't just one thing. It was everything," I answered. Aaron took another sip of his beer. I continued, "It was how you said things. It's like a switch just flipped and it was to hell with me. You were cold and rude. You spoke to me like I mean nothing to you."

Aaron sat his bottle of beer down and leaned towards me, pressing the palms of his hands down on the kitchen island. He hesitated before he spoke to me. "Jada, for the past couple of weeks you've been acting as if I mean nothing to you. I'm sorry if I hurt your feelings with something that I said, but I don't know what you want from me. I've apologized to you. I sent flowers and different gifts to your condo, your restaurant, the salon ... anywhere I thought you might be. I have tried to communicate that my feelings for you are real, but I am who I am. If you can't accept that, I don't know what to tell you."

We sat there in silence for a few more moments before I spoke.

"When did you find out that your father was a drug dealer?" I asked.

Aaron stood up straight with a confused look. "What? Jada, that doesn't have anything to do with –"

"Answer my question, please."

"I don't know," Aaron said, shrugging his shoulders. "I think I always suspected something, but I didn't know for sure until I was like ten. Why?"

"How did you find out?"

"I walked in on a business conversation between my dad and my grandfather. Later my dad sat me down and told me what was up," he answered.

I took another sip of my wine. "I was eight years old. My dad's best friend was killed, and it turned out that the people who did it were really after my father. My mother was scared shitless. So, my parents ended up getting into the biggest argument in the middle of the night. They woke the whole house with their shouting. I can still remember some of the things they said to each other that night," I told him. "The thing I remember most was my mother's concern – not only for her husband's life but also those of her children. My mom told my dad that all the money in the world could never take the place of the ones she loved the most. She didn't want to spend her life looking over her shoulder or worrying about if someone was going to kill her husband or her kids because of what he did for a living."

The frustration disappeared from Aaron's face and his eyes turned sympathetic.

"My dad promised her that she didn't have to worry about that because he would always do everything in his power to protect us," I stated.

"He's done that."

"All his effort didn't save Deuce's life," I said evenly. "Aaron, the thing is ... I never wanted to be in that position either. I can't help the life that I was born into, but I can choose the life I want as an adult. I could have knowingly dated several people that were associated with my father's business, but I chose not to. I thought Israel was a safe bet, but it turned out that he was so closely associated with people that were associated with my dad that it ruined anything we could have ever had. Do you get it now? Do you understand why I've been so upset? You withheld who you were and that took away my ability to make an informed decision before I fell for you."

Aaron walked around the island to where I was standing. He turned my stool around so that I faced him.

"I can't change who I am, and unfortunately I can't change what happened to your brother," he said. "I understand your concern, but you have to let me show you that I'm different from anyone you've ever dealt with in the past. I'll sure that you're always protected. I'm not going to let you go through any of that shit you went through before, but you gotta show me that this is what you want. I love you, but I can't waste time chasing you if you don't want to be caught."

"What did you say?"

"I'm not going to keep chasing you if you don't want to be caught."

"No. Not that."

My lips started to pull into a smile.

"What?" he asked.

"You said you love me," I said.

Aaron rolled his eyes. "Jada, I've told you that before."

I shook my head. "No. You haven't."

"Of course I love you. Do you think I would be dealing with this drama with any other woman when –"

"You better not tell me how you can find my replacement again," I said in a firm tone.

Aaron laughed and shook his head. "Nah. I was going to say that I wouldn't deal with this drama from any other woman when I have all this other work-related shit going on right now."

Aaron took my hands, interlocking his fingers with mine. "I love you. I want to be with you. I've been trying to do everything within reason to show you that. I'm not Israel Mann or anybody else that you're used to. All the drama of your past is over with," he said. "Do whatever you need to do to let that hurt go so you can quit fighting me and let me love you. If the past few weeks have shown you anything, you should know that I'm not going anywhere ... but you have to let me know if this is what you want."

I nodded my head. "I love you too," I said, "and I do want this."

My anger and frustration from the previous weeks seemed to disappear as I realized that he was the one that my heart wanted. I grabbed his shirt and pulled his body close to mine. Aaron leaned down and kissed me on the lips, pulling me up from my stool and into his embrace. I wrapped an arm around his neck and caressed the side of his face while I continued to kiss him back with passion. When he pulled away from me, I was breathless. He kissed me on the forehead and then smacked my ass.

"Let's finish this upstairs."

CAMERON

ONE MONTH LATER

*T*he warmth of the late October air was so pleasant that I drove with my windows down. My vehicle was unusually quiet as I made my way to my destination. Normally I would have music blasting, but that day I preferred the silence as a million thoughts were running through my mind. From business, to Shannon, to Brianna, to Aaron and Jada – my mind was going a million miles per minute.

My father was gone for close to two months, and Aaron and I were no closer to being on better terms. I knew the tension between us was mostly my doing. I didn't appreciate being kept in the dark while Aaron and my father worked out the details of their plan. I also resented everyone thinking I needed help to keep the Atlanta operation afloat. In the back of my mind, I knew there may have been some truth to their thought, because even with Aaron in town things were not running smoothly. There had been a considerable amount of suspicious activity transpiring that was reminiscent of our issues with KS9. We constantly changed our routine and other logistics of the operation, but almost two months later we were still dealing with the same issues. I was also bothered by Aaron's relationship with

Jada. With everything my sister had been through, the last thing she needed was to be the newest fling of Aaron Mercer.

I shut off the engine after pulling into a parking space between my sisters' vehicles. I hopped out of my ride and walked up to the front door of their store front. The door was unlocked, and I walked right in.

"So, this is the spot, huh?" I asked.

Ayanna and Jada turned towards me. The two appeared to be looking over paint samples. Both smiled and walked over to greet me.

"Yes, this is it," Ayanna answered with a wide smile. "We're about a month away from opening the salon. The Grand Opening event will be Thanksgiving weekend."

"That's what's up," I commented with a smile. "Look at my business-owning sisters. I'm proud of y'all."

Jada smiled. "We're very excited. I expect this to be a huge success."

"It's about time you made it down here to take a look," Ayanna said. "Let me show you around."

I followed Ayanna as she showed me around the different areas of the salon. The salon would be offering a variety of services including hair, nails, and makeup. When Ayanna was finished giving me a tour, we made our way back to the front where Jada was still looking over the paint samples.

"I didn't know exactly where you were located until you sent the address earlier today," I said. "I'm over this way a lot actually. Why don't I take y'all to lunch or dinner sometime next week?"

"Sure," Ayanna responded quickly. "My schedule is pretty wide open so just let me know which day, Little Brother. I won't turn down free food."

I laughed. "Alright bet. What about you, Jada? I know you're a workaholic. Are you going to be able to tear yourself away long enough to join me and Yanni for a meal?"

"Yeah ... maybe," she answered hesitantly. "What day do you have in mind? I'm going to Miami for a few days next week."

My face twisted into a frown. "Why?"

Jada gave me a sideways look. "You know why, Cameron," she said in a frustrated tone.

Jada had expressed her discontentment with the growing tension between Aaron and me on more than one occasion.

"I assume you're going down there with your boy, but why?"

"I didn't think I needed a reason to go on a trip with my boyfriend," she responded, "but if you must know, we're going down there for Halloween. He wants me to meet his family, and we're taking his daughter trick-or-treating."

"His daughter, huh?" I asked. "Isn't it a little early to be playing stepmom? I didn't know y'all were that serious."

Ayanna shook her head. "Cam, don't start with that shit, please."

Jada raised her hand to stop Ayanna while looking directly at me. "It's okay, Yanni," she said. "Cameron, despite your own thoughts, Aaron and I are serious. However, I think you should be more concerned with your own relationship – like why Shannon tells me you're still not coming home every night."

My jaw clenched.

"Why are you and Shannon discussing me in the first place?"

"I like her, Cam. You brought her around the family, and now we've built a friendly bond," Jada responded. "She was upset about how things are going and called me to be a listening ear. You need to be worried about fixing your own relationship instead of questioning mine. Aaron and I are good."

I smirked. "Yeah whatever," I said.

I wondered just how good Jada could possibly be with a man that didn't even reside in Atlanta full-time – a man that could lie to her about who he was for months. She was old enough to know better. If she wanted to get herself into another romantic mess, that was her business.

I turned my attention towards Ayanna. "Alright, Yanni. Since the Trap Queen here is going to be kicking it with the Mercers next week, I'll take you to lunch on Tuesday. There's a new hibachi spot down the block I want to check out."

"Sounds good to me," Ayanna said. "I'll be here."

"Bet," I said as my phone started to ring. "Hold on one second."

I stepped away from my sisters to answer my call.

"Zo, what's up?" I asked.

"Aye, man, Luke needs you to come over to the spot," Zo answered.

"For what? I don't answer to him," I said. "I'm with my sisters right now. Ain't nobody worried about Luke."

"Cam, for real. They need you over here man," Zo said. "Aaron and Luke both tried to reach you, but you didn't pick up. You need to get over here."

I shut my eyes for a moment while I let out a heavy sigh. It seemed like something new was going wrong every single day.

"Alright, man. Damn," I said. "I'm on my way."

I ended the call and walked back towards my sisters.

"I gotta head out," I told them.

"Seriously?" Ayanna asked. "You just got here."

I shrugged my shoulders and said, "Your sister's new man and his goon have summoned me." Jada rolled her eyes and walked off. "I'll catch y'all later."

I quickly made my way back to my ride and drove over to the new meeting location. It was an unassuming ranch-style house on a full basement in the heart of East Atlanta. When I pulled up, I noticed three cars outside: Zo's Range Rover, Luke's Tahoe, and Aaron's BMW. Shaking my head, I let out a deep breath and started towards the front door.

"Yo," I called to them when I entered the quiet house.

"Down here, man," Zo said from the basement.

I jogged down the stairs to see the trio standing around a

pool table where there were two duffle bags of money sitting on top of it. There were stacks of cash and a money counter resting on top of the pool table as well.

"What's up?" I asked nonchalantly.

"Who did you have picking up the money on the west side of town this week?" Luke asked.

"Carlos and Twan."

Luke frowned. "Who the fuck is Twan?"

My eyebrows creased into a frown as well. I didn't like being questioned. It was one thing to take direction from Aaron. I accepted it because of who his father was the agreement that was made with my father. Luke wasn't part of that agreement, and I for damn sure did not like being questioned by him.

"One of the guys I have working with Carlos and Dre," I answered.

"Where did he come from?"

I shrugged my shoulders. "He's a friend of Dre's."

Aaron, who was texting on his cell phone, cut his eyes towards me with a questioning look. He opened his mouth to speak for the first time since I entered the house.

"Aye Cam, I don't think it's a good idea to add any new people into the mix right now," he stated.

"Someone has to pick the money up," I countered. "For the most part I trust our dealers, but I wasn't about to send Carlos on a money run by himself."

"Then maybe you should have gone with him or sent someone else. We don't need any new variables right now," Aaron said. "Not until we really get to the bottom of what's been going on around here."

"Technically, your man Luke is a new variable as far as the team is concerned," I responded.

Luke shook his head and exhaled a cloud of smoke before pulling his blunt away from his lips.

I continued to speak to Aaron. "But do you mind telling me why there's such an issue with the people I'm putting on?"

"Because I'm pretty convinced that your boys are up to some shady shit," Aaron responded with a frown. "The count has been short for two weeks in a row. I got a major problem when the money isn't right."

Now I was the one with the frown. "The count has been short like how?" I asked unconvinced.

"Last week the take on the west side was short by ten G's," Aaron responded. "This week it was short by twenty. There doesn't need to be a thirty-stack shortage next week, bruh."

"And for some reason, you think it's Carlos?"

"It's either the new kid you just put on or one of your west side dealers – people that's been working for your family for years. So, you tell me," Aaron said, casually shrugging his shoulders.

"I ain't saying shit, because unlike you two," I said, pointing between Luke and Aaron, "I don't jump to conclusions. I'll get to the bottom of it though. You can bet that."

"You do that," Luke said, "because if you don't handle it, it's going to be out of your hands. You and your people probably won't like my approach if I have to step in and clean up your shit."

Ignoring Luke, I spoke directly to Aaron. "Alright, man. Is this the only reason why you called me down here?"

Aaron shook his head.

"Nah, man. We need to tighten up on who is coming in and out of here," he said. "There's a reason why there's only five keys."

I leaned my head to the side and stared at him.

"There's not supposed to be anyone in here without the five of us, and this damn sure ain't no place for outsiders," Aaron said firmly. "This ain't no damn hangout spot. If it ain't about business, it doesn't need to happen in here. Find somewhere else to socialize."

I let out an irritated sigh. I knew what Aaron was talking about. I had, on more than one occasion, invited a few friends over while I was handling business. I even brought Shannon by the spot one time when we were on our way to get something to eat. Instead of questioning him or letting my frustration show any further, I shrugged my shoulders.

"Got it, boss. No more outsiders."

"Alright, man. That's it," Aaron said, "but for all of our sake, put someone else on the money next week."

"You got it, boss."

Without saying goodbye, I turned and headed towards the stairs. I pulled away from the house with my jaw tight. I would get to the bottom of the issues with the money, but not at the direction of Aaron Mercer. I was my own man and would handle my own business.

JADA

*F*rom the moment we stepped off the plane, I sensed a change in Aaron's spirit. I fell in love with the man I met in Atlanta, but it was clear that Miami was home for him. Since we would only be in Miami for a few days, we didn't have any checked bags – opting only to carry our Louis Vuitton duffle bags. Shouldering both bags, Aaron held my hand and led the way through the airport in search of his driver, Julio. When he found him, he introduced us immediately.

"Julio, my man, what's good?" Aaron greeted with a hug. "This is my lady, Jada."

"I've heard so much about you already, Ms. Reid," Julio said as he shook my hand. "Pleasure to meet you."

"Nice to meet you as well, Julio," I said with a warm smile. "You can just call me Jada."

"Very well, Jada. Aaron, let me get those bags," Julio said as he took our things. "Let's head to the car."

Aaron and I followed Julio as he led us out of the airport to an all-black Escalade. Julio opened my door before putting the bags in the trunk. Aaron helped me into the vehicle and slid next to me.

"Where to?" Julio asked after he climbed behind the wheel.

"We made it in too late to surprise Olivia at school, so just head on to the house," Aaron responded.

Julio pulled away from the curb and started our drive. Aaron wrapped an arm around my shoulders, pulling my body close to his.

"Man, I feel like I haven't been home in forever," he said. "I'm glad you could come meet my family. They're gonna love you."

I smiled at him. "I hope so."

"You sound nervous."

"Not so much about meeting your parents or your sisters," I stated. "I'm just a little nervous about meeting Olivia."

Aaron gave me a confused smile. "Don't be. She's going to love you," he said, kissing my forehead.

"I guess we'll see," I said.

I settled against Aaron and rested my head on his chest. A little tired from our travel and a poor night of rest the previous night, I closed my eyes and quickly nodded off. I was awakened by Aaron gently shaking my shoulder as Julio pulled up to the gate of the Mercer estate.

"Hey, we're here."

Julio entered the security code, and I sat up and looked around. While he pulled into the gate and continued his drive towards the house, I took in my surroundings. The grounds were filled with lush green landscaping and palm trees. Everything was beautiful. I was absolutely speechless. The modern style, waterfront mansion was captivating due to both its size and design. Julio pulled the Escalade to a stop in the circular driveway right at the bottom of the steps that led to the front door. Excited, Aaron quickly opened the door and slid out of the truck. He helped me down and started towards the entrance.

Before Aaron could put his key in the door, it swung open and we were greeted by his mother, Sophia Ramirez Mercer.

"Mijo!" she exclaimed.

"Ma, how did you even know we were here?" Aaron laughed.

Sophia pulled Aaron into a tight hug. She was just as beautiful as her pictures. She was a tall woman, standing at about five foot ten with an olive skin complexion and thick, brown hair that was cut and styled into a shoulder-length bob. She had a slim figure, and it was obvious that she took great care with her appearance. Sophia looked much younger than her mid-fifties age.

"I told security to let me know when you pulled up to the gate."

Sophia kissed him on the cheek and released him from her embrace. Her smile widened when she turned to me. She pulled me into a tight embrace as well. When she let me go, she patted my cheek and said, "Oh Jada ... I haven't seen you in ages. Look at you all grown up! You are beautiful. Just like your mother."

"Thank you," I said with a wide smile of my own.

"Come on inside. Both of you," Sophia said as she took us by the hands. "Everyone is here."

I was silent as we followed Sophia into the house. The inside was just as gorgeous as the outside. It took a lot to impress me, but the Mercer property definitely did that. All of our attention was diverted when we heard the sound of feet running down the hallway.

"Daddy!" I heard Olivia squeal as she ran full speed towards Aaron.

Olivia resembled her grandmother Sophia with similar facial features, the same olive complexion, and thick brown hair styled in two pigtail braids. She was still dressed in her school uniform. Aaron scooped her up into a big hug.

"Hey, baby," he greeted her with a kiss on the cheek. "What did I tell you about running in the house?"

Olivia covered her face with her hands. "I know. No running

in the house. I'm just happy to see you. I didn't know if you were going to make it," she said.

"I'm happy to see you too. I told you I will be here to take you trick-or-treating with your cousins," Aaron said as he kissed her on the cheek again and sat her back down on her feet. He looked at me. "Olivia, I want you to meet someone."

Olivia smiled in my direction. "You must be Jada," she said. "It's very nice to meet you."

"It's even nicer to meet you too," I said, shaking her little hand.

"Want to see my costume?" she asked me.

"Of course."

I left Sophia and Aaron to chat amongst themselves and followed Olivia to her bedroom. After a few minutes of admiring Olivia's Disney princess costume, Aaron joined us.

"Livy, let me take Jada to meet your grandpa and your aunts," he said as he wrapped an arm around my shoulders. "Dinner will be ready in a little bit."

Aaron steered me out of the room and towards the back of the house. We made our way out to the veranda where the rest of the family was gathered poolside. Aaron's father was the first to greet me. I easily saw why anyone would be intimidated by Manny Mercer. Aaron and Manny shared similar facial features, but Manny's complexion was more of a chestnut skin tone. He sported similar facial hair as his son and the same thick eyebrows although his hair was a salt and pepper mix. He was as tall as my father, towering over my five-foot seven frame. Manny had a serious face but sported a wide grin and extended his arms to embrace me.

"My goodness, I haven't seen you since you were a little girl," he greeted me when we pulled away from our hug. "It's nice to see you, Jada. We're happy to have you in our home, and I'm pleased to hear that you've been keeping my son company and out of trouble."

"I'm certainly trying," I responded with a laugh.

Aaron motioned towards his sisters, Regina and Daniella. "Jada, these are my sisters. Gigi ... Dani ... this is Jada."

It's funny how genetics work. None of the Mercer siblings actually looked like siblings. At the age of thirty-five, Regina was two years older than Aaron and almost a younger spitting image of their mother – including her height, body build, and facial features. From her roots, I could tell that her thick, dark brown hair was not as fine as Sophia's, but it was straightened and hung down her back. She flashed a tight smile and waved in my direction before turning her attention back towards her children, eight-year-old twin girls who were playing in the backyard.

Aaron's younger sister, Daniella, just turned twenty-three and was set to graduate from the University of Miami in a matter of weeks. As far as appearances were concerned, she was almost the complete opposite of Regina. Daniella was an inch or two shorter than me with a skin tone closer to their father's. Her physique was much more voluptuous than that of her mother and older sister. Her hair was black, thick, and curly, much like mine, and resting on her shoulders. She got up from her chair and walked towards me with a wide smile on her heart-shaped face.

"Hey, Jada!" she greeted me warmly. "It's nice to meet you! I'm glad you could make the trip."

"Thank you. I'm glad to be here."

"Have you gotten settled in yet? Do you want anything to drink?" Daniella asked. "Dinner will be ready in about an hour or so, and then the kids will be going trick-or-treating around seven."

"Julio took the bags up to the room, but we haven't been up there yet," Aaron answered.

"And I'm fine. Thank you for asking. Just a little tired. I may try to sneak a quick nap before dinner," I said.

"Of course," Manny said. "Son, show her to your room. If you want to relax too, that's fine. You and I can chat later. I'll have someone alert you when dinner is ready."

"Cool."

I was quiet while Aaron led me back into the house and towards an elevator. When we reached the top level of the house, I followed Aaron down the hallway where he opened the door to his room. I stepped inside and once again was blown away by the size and décor of the room. Immediately upon entering the room, we were standing in a sitting room the size of the common area in my condo. Through an arched doorway, I could see his bedroom, and I headed right for the California king-sized bed, kicking off my shoes and sliding under the covers. Aaron followed me, stepping out of his shoes, and sitting on top of the covers next to me.

He ran his fingers through my hair, tucking a few strands behind my ear. "You feeling alright?"

I nodded. "Just a little tired. I'm glad we got away from Atlanta, even if only for a couple of days. I feel like I've been running myself ragged trying to get everything together for the salon's grand opening in a few weeks. I'm just starting to feel exhausted."

"The grand opening will be here before you know it," he said. "Just about three more weeks."

I nodded. He was right. In a few short weeks all the hard work Ayanna and I put in would pay off when we opened our new salon and spa. I couldn't wait to debut my new business, but in the meantime, I needed rest. I closed my eyes for another nap beside my man before dinner.

AARON

Family dinner and trick-or-treating had come and gone, and it was late into the evening. I sat on the veranda with my father enjoying the ocean view, the night air, and a stiff drink. My parents stayed home while Dani, Gigi, Jada, and I took the kids out. Despite Regina being Regina – cold and uninviting – the night had been successful and the ladies in my life were starting to bond. After we returned with the kids, Regina left to go home. Owning a house not too far away with her husband, Regina was the only one who did not live at the family estate. The house was built with the intention to accommodate the whole family, and it had worked out to my benefit. Traveling as much as I did and having more than enough space in the family home, I never saw the need to move out. Staying at my parents' estate also provided Olivia with a sense of stability since she was often in my mother's care when I was out of town.

I watched my father while he lit a cigar. "How's everything going in Atlanta?" he asked casually.

I considered my response before I spoke. I had not shared all the details with him about my recent troubles with the Reid organization and the new guys that Cameron had brought on board. However, I knew better than to bullshit him. My father could have received information from anyone at any time. There was no telling how much he really knew. I shrugged my shoulders.

"Cameron hasn't quite come around like Julian expected him too. He's still providing more resistance than I would like," I answered, "and he and Luke are always bumping heads."

"How long are you going to let that continue, and is it affecting the bottom line?" he asked.

"You know I don't really have that much patience, but I've been trying to keep it cool with Cameron because of Julian," I answered. "Julian's mom isn't doing well, but he'll be back at some point. I ain't trying to disrupt things too much."

My father shrugged his shoulders and released a cloud of smoke from his lips. "I don't know about that."

"About what?" I asked. "About me not disturbing things?"

He shook his head.

"No. I don't know about Julian coming back to the business," my dad answered. "After the way things unfolded with Caleb Bridges and KS9, it's my understanding that he's no longer in the good graces of the mayor and the police chief. Also, Deuce's death has been really hard on him. He never really mourned his wife, and now he's about to lose his mother as well. He's mentioned retiring from this business altogether. I think that may be a bigger possibility than we initially believed."

"Damn. You really think he's going to step away from the life that he's spent over thirty years building?" I asked.

My father shrugged his shoulders. "I think we need to be prepared for anything."

"Who would even run the Atlanta market? Deuce is gone, and we can't give Cameron that type of responsibility. Not yet, and not any time soon from the shit I've been seeing," I stated.

"That's something we would have to figure out," my dad answered. "How do you like Atlanta?"

I gave him a confused look. I never gave him any indication that I wanted to live anywhere besides Miami.

"Atlanta is cool. I know the city pretty well, but Miami is home," I told him. "I've never thought about living anywhere else on a permanent basis. I can't see myself moving Olivia away from her family – either side of her family. I haven't discussed it with Jada, but I just assumed when Julian came back that I would return to Miami."

My father brought the cigar back up to his lips and turned to look at our view of the water. "So," he said, pulling the cigar away from his mouth, "you and Julian Reid's baby girl, huh?"

"Pops ... that shit's crazy how it all worked out. I didn't even know who she really was for a couple of months," I responded.

My dad nodded as he continued to look out onto the water. I could tell that he was thinking about something.

"What's on your mind?" I asked.

He shrugged his shoulders in response but then said, "I like her. Your mother and Daniella like her. She's very personable. Respectful. She has a great sense of humor, and she's ambitious. It also doesn't hurt that she's easy on the eyes."

"But?" I asked.

Sometimes I had to pry information out of my father, especially if it was something he thought I might not want to hear.

He turned to make eye contact with me. "I see the way she looks at you, Black. That girl is in love. She's probably picturing her happily ever after with you. I'd bet money Jada's already considering the 'til death do you part,'" he said. "Is that what you want? You haven't been in a serious relationship in quite some time. I just hope you two are on the same page. The last thing we need is for you to be in a messy situation with the youngest daughter of one of our biggest money makers."

I hesitated before responding. He was right. It had been a long time since I entertained a female seriously. Jada was the first woman I brought home to meet my family since Olivia's mother. Luckily, Jada and Isabela were nothing alike.

"I understand where you're coming from. I enjoyed my freedom as a single man, but I'm over that. Jada and I are on the same page. I know it might sound crazy, but I want all that happily ever after shit too. As far as I'm concerned, she's it for me," I told my father.

A smile spread across his face. "Then I wish you two the best. She's definitely brought another side out of you," he said. "A better side. A brighter side. I haven't seen you this happy in a long time."

"I feel the same way."

I hung around the veranda with my father a little while longer until he finished his cigar and we both finished our drinks. I refilled my glass before heading up to the room. It was well after midnight. After our long day, I figured Jada would be asleep once I made it upstairs. However, when I entered the room, I was surprised to see her on the balcony speaking on the phone. Barefoot in a nightgown, she looked beautiful in the moonlight. I kicked off my shoes in the sitting room and quietly made my way to the balcony door, standing a few feet behind Jada while she continued her conversation. I took a sip from my glass and listened to her speak.

"Ness, Olivia is so sweet and so adorable," I heard her say. "We had so much fun tonight. I'm really glad he brought me down here."

She paused while Vanessa spoke on the other end of the line.

"His family is wonderful. I love them, and their estate is breathtaking," she said. "I mean absolutely gorgeous."

"You're absolutely gorgeous," I said from the doorway.

Jada looked over her shoulder and smiled at me.

"Vanessa, let me call you back tomorrow."

I walked over to her as she ended her call. I took her phone and sat both it and my drink down on the balcony table. She wrapped her arms around my neck while I grabbed her waist and pressed my body against hers, pinning her to the railing.

"I don't think your sister likes me," she said.

"Don't worry about that. Gigi doesn't like anybody. She barely likes herself," I said, kissing her collarbone. "But my mom and Dani love you."

I kissed her neck. "And my dad loves you."

I kissed her lips. "And Olivia loves you."

I looked into her eyes and said, "I love you."

"I love you too," she said with a smile.

My lips met with hers again and she kissed me deeply while my hands caressed her body, running up and down her curves. I rubbed my hands over her backside, grabbing her behind roughly and discovering through the sheer material of her nightgown that she wasn't wearing any underwear. I felt my manhood growing against her stomach. Jada always turned me on with ease and the brown liquor I drank only heightened my desire for her. I pulled my lips from her mouth, opting to nuzzle her neck and lift her off her feet. She wrapped her legs around my waist. When I sucked on her neck – her spot – a satisfied moan escaped her lips while she rubbed the back of my head and ran her fingers through my hair. She held onto me tightly, and I reached to undo my pants.

"Let's go inside," she said softly.

I shook my head. "Nah. I want you right here," I said into her ear.

Jada placed her hands on my shoulders while I pushed my underwear down.

"Outside? Aaron, what if someone sees us? Or hears us?"

"Sssssh, everybody on this side of the house is already asleep. Ain't nobody gonna see us," I told her as I rubbed myself against her opening. She was wet and tight. I wanted her right then and there. "Just make sure you keep quiet, so you don't wake nobody up."

"Aaron," she moaned my name while I held onto her waist and slid her down onto my erection. Her walls were tight as I stroked her slowly. She moaned again. "Oh my God."

"You scared?" I asked her.

Jada shook her head while I eased my way further inside of her. She bit down on her bottom lip to stop any further sound from escaping her mouth. Her face displayed her satisfaction. I watched her while she squeezed her muscles around me tighter and rolled her hips towards me, her body rising up and down against mine. With my arms underneath her thighs, I pushed her back against the railing and spread her legs wider so I could go deeper while I increased my pace. Jada placed a hand on my torso in an attempt to keep me at a distance.

"Move your hand," I commanded in a low tone.

She did as she was told but wrapped her arms around my neck and shoulders, holding on to me for dear life. Pounding into her as hard and deep as I could, I was giving her a mixture of pleasure and pain – just how she liked it. The soft sounds escaping her lips were a cross between a moan and a whimper. Everything about her was intoxicating. From the way she looked to the way she smelled to the way she felt when I was inside of her – she had my head spinning. Unable to keep quiet, Jada buried her face into my shoulder to muffle her cries as her body shuddered against mine. Her wetness rained down on me causing my body to tense.

"Uggghhhh ... shit!" I groaned as I let go inside her.

My chest heaved up and down while I fought to catch my breath. Jada kissed my lips before leaning back to look in my eyes.

"I thought we were supposed to be keeping quiet," she said jokingly.

LAUGHING, I RELEASED HER LEGS AND PLACED HER ON HER FEET. I shrugged my shoulders and pulled my pants up. I flashed a half-smile and said, "I couldn't help it, mama. That shit was too good."

Jada winked at me. "I know it was," she said arrogantly. "Come shower with me before we lay down."

She took my hand and started back into the room. As I walked behind her, I shook my head and stared at her in amazement. I didn't know how she had gotten ahold of me, but she had. I knew in that moment that there wasn't anything I wouldn't do to protect her and make sure that she stayed mine.

LUKE

*W*hile Aaron was in Miami with his family, I hoped for a quiet Friday night. Most of the day's business was wrapped up, and I had actually made it back to my spot at a decent time. The only business remaining of the day was Cameron's team collecting the money on the west side of town. Months ago, when Aaron informed me that we were going to Atlanta for an extended period of time, I decided to lease a loft downtown. I needed a stable place to rest my head and being in the city put me a whole lot closer to the action than Aaron. If something unexpected happened, I could roll up quickly.

Anticipating a quiet weekend for the first time in months, I flew my girlfriend, Nakia, up from Miami to spend a few days with me. She was cooking dinner while I lounged on the couch watching sports. All I could think about was how thankful I was for a moment of peace. If Aaron had told me what I was signing up for by following him to Atlanta, I probably would have tried to find a way to weasel out of it. It seemed like Julian Reid's team couldn't do anything right. Every day there was a new problem, and I was starting to lose my patience.

"I'm almost finished," Nakia called from the kitchen. "The greens will be done in just a moment."

My mouth was watering from the smell of the dinner she prepared. I couldn't wait to taste the baked chicken, macaroni and cheese, and collard greens. I stood up from the sofa to wash my hands but heard my phone rang. I sighed heavily before snatching up the phone to see Zo's name on the caller ID.

"Man, don't tell me the take on the west side is short again," I said into the phone without a proper greeting.

"Luke, it ain't short," he said. "It's gone."

"The fuck?!" I asked in a frustrated tone. "What do you mean it's gone?"

Zo let out a heavy sigh. "I was riding with JB and Carlos. After the last stop, we headed to drop the money off. We were taking it to the warehouse until tomorrow, but some niggas were waiting on us when we got there," he said. "Hopped out of a truck and started shooting. JB got hit. The money got jacked."

"All of it?" I asked for clarification.

"Every single dime."

I shook my head. We were definitely talking about more than six figures. If Aaron was pissed about the ten and twenty thousand-dollar losses over the last couple of weeks, he was going to lose his mind about a loss that totaled well over a hundred thousand dollars.

"Where is JB now?" I asked Nakia starting to make our plates. I shook my head in frustration because I knew I would not be eating anytime soon.

"I drove him over to Julian's doctor."

In my mind, I already knew the answer to my next question, but I asked it anyway.

"Zo, let me ask you something," I started. "Normally, when the money is picked up, it comes to the house. If you all had an unexpected final destination this evening, how the fuck was someone already waiting on you?"

91

"I don't know, man. I mean ... we were the only ones that knew where we were taking the money. I ain't said shit to no one," Zo answered.

I smirked. "I doubt JB did either if he's the one that got shot. Where is Carlos?"

"Still in the car. Just left JB at the doc," Zo responded.

"Head over to the meeting spot," I instructed him. "Don't tell him that I'm on my way."

"Bet."

I ended the call and turned towards Nakia.

"It's okay, baby," she said. "I'll wrap your plate up for you so you can have something to eat when you get back."

Nakia had been with me long enough to understand that the fewer questions she asked the better off she would be. She was just the type of woman that a man like me needed. I grabbed my keys and gave her a quick kiss.

"Lock up and put the alarm on," I told her. "I'll let you know when I'm on my way back."

On the way down to my truck, I sent a text to Blue, PO, and Cameron telling them to meet me at the meeting house in East Atlanta. When I pulled up Blue and PO were already on the porch waiting for me.

"Where's Cameron?" I asked.

"He said he's on the way," PO answered.

"What's going on?" Blue asked.

"I'm about to find out," I said, heading into the house.

PO and Blue followed me as I headed into the house and directly towards the basement. Carlos and Zo were on the couch watching TV, and Carlos was texting on his phone. Startling everyone in the room, I snatched Carlos off of the sofa, holding him by the collar of his shirt while I slammed him against the wall. His cell phone fell out of his hand and onto the floor.

"Yo Luke! What the hell?" Carlos asked, looking at me with wide eyes.

"Who you been working with?" I shouted.

"Huh? What are you talking about?" Carlos asked.

"You're the common factor in a lot of the money problems that we've had around here," I said. I slammed his body into the wall again. "So, we're onto whatever slick shit you've been doing. I'm going to ask you one more time. Who have you been working with? Who did you tell about the drop tonight?"

"I don't know what you're talking about man," Carlos said. "For real, Luke. I was with JB and Zo all night. I ain't talk to anybody."

"You think I'm fucking stupid," I barked at him, slamming his body against the wall once more. I turned to look at Blue. "Give me his phone."

Blue moved towards Carlos's phone.

"Luke, man, what are you doing?" Carlos asked.

I removed one hand from around Carlos's neck to get his phone from Blue. I tried to access the phone, but it was locked. I pulled my other hand from around Carlos's neck and held the phone towards him while pulling my gun from my waistband with my other hand.

"Unlock the phone."

Carlos did not reach for the phone. "Ain't shit in there. I don't know what you're looking for."

I shook my head and laughed. I turned towards Blue and PO. "This nigga really thinks I'm stupid," I said with a laugh.

Without warning, I turned around and pistol-whipped Carlos, knocking him down on the floor.

"Fuck!" Carlos screamed as his hands went towards his face. Blood flowed from his mouth and his nose.

I squatted next to his body. "Look, man, I ain't in the mood to keep going back and forth with you," I said. "This shit pulled me out of my house and away from my woman on what was supposed to be a peaceful, quiet night. Now if there's nothing to hide in the phone, then you shouldn't have a problem doing what the fuck I told you to do and unlocking that bitch."

I tossed the phone at him, but he continued to cradle his face. Carlos stared at me for a moment. When his eyes traveled down to the pistol in my hand, he reached for his cellphone. I heard the front door open and close. Cameron had finally shown up. Carlos put in his passcode, unlocked the phone, and handed it back to me.

I was standing up when Cameron made his way into the basement.

"What the hell is going on?" Cameron asked.

I ignored him. While Zo filled Cameron in on the events of the evening, I went to Carlos's call log. It was empty. I narrowed my eyes at him. If he truly had nothing to hide, he wouldn't have deleted his call log. I looked back at the phone and found his messaging app and shook my head when I opened it. His dumbass forgot to erase his texts. The suspicions that Aaron and I had were confirmed as I thumbed through the text messages in Carlos's phone.

"Luke, what's going on?" Cameron questioned after Zo brought him up to speed.

"This," I told him. "This is what's going on."

I tossed the phone to Cameron so he could see what I saw. Carlos had been texting two different contacts in his phone – MP1 and MP2 – for a while. The message exchanges explained a lot about the issues we had been having for months. Most importantly whoever MP1 and MP2 were, they had been behind the evening's robbery. They had our money.

Cameron scrolled through the messages with his frown becoming increasingly more intense.

"Cam, man ... I can explain," Carlos stated. He was still balled up in pain on the floor.

Cameron looked from the phone to Carlos. Without saying

anything to him, Cameron pulled his gun out and fired three shots into Carlos's body – two in the chest and one in the head.

"Cameron, *what the fuck?*" I shouted.

Cameron turned towards Blue and said, "Call the cleanup crew and get his ass out of here."

Blue shook his head in disbelief, but pulled his phone out and placed the call. PO walked over to where Cameron and I were standing.

"Cam, was that really the right move to make?" PO questioned.

Cameron turned his frown on PO. "Was there any other move to make?" he asked. "This motherfucker has been robbing us blind for months. Did you think I was going to let his ass live?"

"We still don't know what the hell MP stands for!" I shouted to Cameron. "We know Carlos had something to do with the losses true. What else do you know, smart guy? You just killed the nigga without any answers!"

"Fuck that!" Cameron spat. "I wouldn't trust anything that came out of his mouth. There are numbers associated with the contacts in the phone. You and Manny Jr. can figure that shit out."

"*Excuse you?*" I asked him with a sideways look.

"Carlos was a problem, so I handled that," Cameron said, taking a step closer to me. PO moved to place an arm between us, making sure that we kept our distance from each you and Aaron come up here to handle shit, right? So, handle it. You get paid enough money to do a little detective work."

I smirked and shook my head at Cameron in response. I couldn't believe that the man standing in front of me was the son of Julian Reid. From what I had seen in the prior months, Cameron was nothing like his father. Julian was disciplined, careful, and smart. Cameron always seemed to be the loudest, most disrespectful person in the room. If he had been anyone else's son, there's no way that Aaron nor I would have tolerated his shit for as long as we had. I knew that the patience was running thin on my end. I was certain that when I called Aaron, there would be no more Mr. Nice Guy whether he dated Cameron's sister or not.

With my eyes on him the whole time, I watched Cameron leave the basement. I pulled my phone from my pocket.

"Aye, man, what's up?" Aaron answered the phone.

His tone was jovial, and I could hear Jada laughing in the background. Too bad I had to be the one to ruin his mood.

"Black, you ain't gonna believe this shit ..."

AARON

*T*hree weeks had passed. Three weeks since Jada met my folks. Three weeks since Cameron killed Carlos. Three weeks since I made a major shift in the way I conducted business in Atlanta. It was obvious that Cameron couldn't be trusted to handle anything of importance. Luke and I shared our suspicions about Cameron's new guys months prior, but he brushed us off with indifference. Not only were we right, but in the time it took the truth to come to light we had taken a loss of over a quarter million dollars. There was no way I could allow that to continue.

After a conversation with my father and a vague explanation to Julian, Cameron was stripped of any real power he once held. Nothing happened in Atlanta unless Luke or I knew gave approval. Cameron had no direct reports. Everyone answered to me – Cameron included. That did not go over well with him, but he had no choice.

I headed to the East Atlanta meeting house on my way to Jada's grand opening event at her salon. I looked forward to celebrating her new venture by her side, but duty called. When I pulled up to the house, I parked on the street and quickly made my way inside to the basement. Everyone I was expecting to be present was already there, including Cameron. I approached Luke.

"I'm surprised you're here," Luke said. "Isn't your girl's thing about to start?"

I nodded. "Yeah. My mom and Dani came up to show support, and they are already over there," I answered. "I'm headed that way next."

"Cool. Everyone is ready to go," Luke told me. "All the money should be picked up and brought back here before five. Then the dealers are going to be picking up their product from the tire warehouse after eight. PO and Zo are going to be here to make sure that the money is right when it's dropped off. I'll be at the warehouse with Blue."

"So, everything's good?" I asked.

Luke nodded. "Everything's good."

I glanced over at Cameron. "What is he doing?"

"I don't know. I thought he would be going to his sister's grand opening, but he's sticking around here. I guess he'll be here with PO. As long as he stays quiet and out of the way, I really don't give a shit," Luke answered.

"Bet. I'll probably swing back by here after Jada's event to make sure everything's good with the money," I told him. "I know you can hold it down at the other spot."

"For sure," Luke agreed.

"Alright, man. Let me get out of here then," I said as I slapped hands with my friend, "but let me know if there are any problems."

Luke agreed, and I was on my way. It was a short drive to Jada and Ayanna's salon. When I arrived, the event was just getting under way. Potential clients were invited to enjoy champagne and hors d'oeuvres while meeting the staff and getting familiar with the services that were offered. Jada and Ayanna's marketing team had done a good job getting the word out, and there were a few local reporters and bloggers present to cover the event.

I made my way inside and was not surprised to see my mother and sister already getting manicures. As much as they cared about appearances, I expected nothing less. Spotting Jada posing for a few photos across the room, I grabbed two glasses of champagne and made my way over to her.

"Hey mama," I greeted her with a kiss on the cheek.

"Baby," she said with a wide smile on her face, "I'm glad you're here."

"There's nowhere else I'd rather be right now. I'm proud of you."

I took a sip of champagne and extended the other glass towards her. She shook her head and ran her hands down the front of her dress instead of taking the glass from my hands.

"None for me. Thank you," she said.

"You sure?"

"Yeah. I think it's just all the excitement from today, but my stomach is in knots right now. I don't think champagne is going to help," she said with a slight laugh.

"More for me then," Ayanna said as she approached us from my left.

I handed her the glass and greeted her with a hug.

"Hey Aaron," she said. "I just love your mom and your sister! How long are they going to be in town?"

"They actually just flew up for the day. They'll be headed home tonight."

"They are so sweet. I had to treat them to manicures on the house," Ayanna told me. "Now that you're here ... maybe you can get my sister to get somewhere and sit her butt down."

"Yanni, I'm fine," Jada tried to dismiss her sister.

"What's wrong?" I asked.

"She hasn't eaten all day, and she's been running around here like a chicken with its head cut off even though she doesn't feel well," Ayanna answered.

I looked at Jada who rolled her eyes at Ayanna before turning to look at me.

"I'm fine," she repeated.

"Uh-huh. Tell us anything." Ayanna said. "I'm going to call our brother and see why he isn't here."

When Ayanna walked away, I turned back towards Jada. "What's really going on?" I asked her.

"Nothing," Jada answered as she gave me a quick kiss on the lips.

She forced a smile onto her face, but I could see right through her charade. I wasn't going to push the issue in the middle of her event, but I made a note to follow up later.

"Alright. I'mma let it go, but at least put something in your mouth," I urged her. "The last thing you want is for these bloggers to get pictures of you passed out because you didn't eat."

"Baby, I will get something in a moment. I promise," she said with the same forced smile, "but right now let me introduce you to some people."

I didn't protest and Jada took my hand, leading me through the crowd and introducing me to various staff members. I was thankful for Luke. If he had not been in Atlanta, I would not have the free time for such moments. Knowing that he was readily available to oversee things was a huge relief. Luckily, things had gone smoothly since Carlos was taken care of. It was my hope things continued to go well, and that MP1 and MP2 had disappeared for good.

JADA

I shifted under the weight of the arm Aaron had securely wrapped around my midsection. After we left the salon, he left to check on business, but met me at my condo around ten o'clock that night. I was thankful that he was there with me to celebrate the events of the day. After continuing our celebration in the bedroom, Aaron was sleeping peacefully while I had been awake for hours. My eyes wandered over to the clock on my bedside table. It was almost five o'clock in the morning. I closed my eyes tightly and sighed heavily. I had an interview and photo shoot with Atlanta Magazine in a matter of hours. My mind was running all night long, and I wasn't sure if I was going to get any sleep. I could feel the weight of the bags under my eyes.

Carefully, I managed to free myself from Aaron's embrace without waking him. I slipped out of the bed and picked my nightgown up from the floor, slipping it on over my head. Grabbing my Louis Vuitton tote, I crept into my master bathroom. I closed the door behind me and placed my purse on the counter. For a moment, I stood in the dark, palms down on the cold marble counter. Refusing to look at my reflection in the mirror, I hung my head as I took a couple of deep breaths.

After a moment, I reached over to flip on the light. Still avoiding my reflection, I fished through my purse until my hands rested on the item I was looking for. I purchased the First Response pregnancy test three days before and had carried it in my purse ever since. I wanted to tell myself that with the excitement of the grand opening I had not found the right time to take the test. However, that was a lie. It was probably truer that I was avoiding taking the test, because I wasn't sure I was ready to face the results. I had exhibited signs even before Aaron took me to meet his family. In all honesty, I had a pretty good idea what the outcome would be.

I ripped the box and revealed the test in its individual wrapping. Without hesitation, I removed it from the package. Holding the stick in my hand, I paused for a brief moment before moving to the toilet. I pulled down my underwear and sat down on the toilet. When I was finished, I put the test on the counter and started to wait.

Thirty seconds ...

After staring at the stick for half a minute, I turned on the hot water and washed my hands thoroughly. I switched the water from hot to cold and splashed my face. I finally looked into the mirror and stared at my reflection, frowning at my bloodshot eyes. The makeup artist was going to have a hell of a time trying to make me look presentable. I sighed and ran my fingers through my loose, disheveled hair.

Sixty seconds ...

I turned away from the mirror and leaned against the counter for support. I felt nauseous for somewhere around the hundredth time in the last 24 hours. In another minute I would probably have confirmation of my suspicion. Things would possibly change forever. I shook my head and let out a slight laugh at how much my life could change in such a small window of time.

Ninety seconds ...

I couldn't believe that I was in this position again. Of course, I knew I could have and maybe should have been more careful. Yet there I was. So much of my future was undefined and revolving around the man that was peacefully sleeping in my bedroom. There was no doubt in my heart that I was in love with him. I could tell just from looking in could come our way.

Two minutes.

I took in a sharp breath and turned back around. When my eyes rested on the test, I saw that my suspicion was confirmed. I was pregnant. Again. The air drained from my lungs and my eyes started to water. I struggled to catch my breath as another strong wave of nausea hit me. It was all I could do to rush back to the toilet before the vomit escaped my mouth.

A few moments later, I was on my hands and knees in front of the toilet when I heard knocking on the bathroom door.

"Babe ... is everything okay in there?" Aaron's asked sleepily.

Still crouched down on the floor, I couldn't respond. I shut my eyes tightly as my sobs overtook me. After hearing my cries, Aaron opened the door.

"Jada, what's going on?" he asked with a voice full of concern as he stepped into the bathroom.

His eyes widened when he saw me on the floor. He started in my direction until I pointed towards the counter. His eyes shifted towards the sink and rested on the pregnancy test.

He froze.

After a brief hesitation, he stepped over to the counter and picked it up.

"Shit," he mumbled when he read the positive result.

My tears started up again. Aaron tossed the stick back onto the counter and rushed towards me.

"Hey, come here," he said in a comforting tone. He picked me up from the floor, taking me into his arms.

Aaron sat on the edge of the tub with me on his lap. He brushed my hair out of my face and wiped the tears from my face.

"What's all the crying for?"

"I'm sorry," I said, my eyes still watery.

"For what?" Aaron asked. He kissed me on the bridge of my nose. "You didn't do this by yourself."

I shrugged my shoulders. "I know ... but I feel like the timing is awful. We both have a lot going on right now, and you said you weren't even sure if you wanted any more children."

"Don't worry about all that, Jada," he said firmly. "What do you want?"

I looked him directly in his eyes. "I don't think I want an abortion."

"I didn't think that you did. Listen, I told you months ago that I wasn't going anywhere. So, whatever you want to do, I'm here for you – both of you," he stated, placing a hand on my stomach. "I'm in love with you. You don't have anything to worry about, mama."

"But I am a little worried," I admitted to him. "Aaron, I've had two miscarriages in the last couple of years. I can't help but to be worried."

"Tell me what I can do to ease your mind?"

"I don't want to tell anybody right now."

Aaron frowned. "What? Why?"

"I just want to keep it between us until I know how far along I am. I want to make sure that everything is okay," I answered. Aaron's facial expression softened. "Please."

Aaron hesitated for a moment but then kissed me on the cheek and rubbed my thigh. "Whatever you want, mama."

I nodded and rested my head on his shoulder for a brief moment. Aaron kissed me on the forehead and placed me on the tub before standing up. I sat on the edge quietly as I watched him clean up the bathroom. He wet a washcloth for me and handed it to me so I could wash my face. He disappeared briefly and then returned with a bottle of water, which he handed to me.

"Are you ready to come back to bed?" he asked, as he extended his hand towards me.

"Yes."

I took his hand and followed him back into bed. I cuddled up to him and laid my head on his chest. I shut my eyes tightly, but I still wasn't sure if I would get any rest. Aaron's words were reassuring, but I knew that neither of us could predict the future. Lying on his back, Aaron had one arm wrapped around my shoulders and his other hand resting behind his head. In the darkness, I peeked at him to see that he was staring at the ceiling with his eyes wide open. It appeared that now he was the one that could not sleep.

MICHAELA

"So, what now, Michaela?" Mikey asked. He paced back and forth in front of me. "They already took out the boy Carlos. I know you don't trust Dre to keep things going by himself."

I continued to file my nails and sit on the sofa in my living room. Mikey had been ranting for a few minutes because we had been thrown a curveball in regard to our plans. For months we had been wreaking havoc and causing discord from DC to Atlanta amongst Julian Reid's organization by way of the two men we had on the inside, Carlos and Dre. Fortunately for us, Cameron Reid had been stupid enough to allow our guys access to sensitive information about their business. That allowed Mikey and I the opportunity to pad our pockets over time, but Mikey and I were not robbers by trade. We were killers. Our goal by instigating the confusion within the Reid organization was to cause enough confusion so that their leaders became unfocused and let their guards down. Then Mikey and I would be able to follow through with our real plan – which was to eliminate Julian Reid.

We were orchestrating moves from behind the scenes for

several months, but it was time to switch things up. The dynamics of our plan were going to have to change with the news that Carlos was killed. Although I was pretty sure that Aaron Mercer and Cameron Reid had no idea that Carlos and Dre had been working for my brother and myself, it was pretty obvious that they knew Carlos was up to something. I needed to rework our strategy. Mikey was right. There was no way I could trust Dre to carry out a job that big by himself. Once Mikey and I worked out the details of our new strategy we were going to have to make our way back down to Atlanta.

I rolled my eyes at him.

"Stop pacing back and forth. You're starting to make me dizzy with all that shit. Obviously, the plan is going to change, Mike," I said, looking up from my nails. "I figured that out without all your stressing."

"Okay. How?"

"For one, Dre can't do it by himself so we're definitely going to have to go back down to Atlanta," I responded.

"When?"

"When we finish working out all the other details," I answered.

Mikey looked at me expectantly. "What does that include? I had no idea this was going to take this long, Michaela."

"Julian's been gone for months, and we have no idea when he'll be back. We're also having trouble locating him because no one really knows where he is. He was very smart to have his mother off the grid. An elderly woman alone on the West coast would have been too easy of a target for us. If we were able to find her, we would be able to find him. So far, we haven't been able to do either," I told him. "We need to change the target."

"To who?"

"If we can't get to Julian, then I say we get to someone close to him," I answered. "We need to take out someone that will make him wish he was dead."

A sinister grin tugged at Mikey's lips. "I like what you're thinking, Sis. Tell me more."

CAMERON

Out of breath and dripping with sweat, Shannon rolled off me and laid beside me in the bed. She pulled the sheets up to her shoulders, covering her naked body as she cozied up to me.

"I'm glad you're back home," she said.

She caressed my chest with her nails, tracing the outlines of my muscles. To be honest, I was happy to be home too. With everything going on with work and my family, I needed the consistency that Shannon provided. Brianna was fun. I hadn't completely ended things with her, but I needed Shannon by my side. I kissed her on the forehead.

"Trust me. I'm glad to be home," I told her.

In the stillness of the room, we both heard my cell phone vibrate. I reached to pick it up from the floor where it had fallen. I looked at the screen to see that Luke was attempting to reach me. I smirked and sat the phone back down.

"Do you need to get that?" Shannon asked.

I shook my head.

"Nah. I ain't fucking with them tonight," I answered. "Besides there ain't shit that we need to discuss anyway."

I pulled away from Shannon and sat up in the bed, swinging my legs over the side. I was trying to spend a peaceful evening with my girl. The last thing I wanted to deal with was work-related bullshit – especially not from Luke. Shannon scooted behind me, rubbing my back before resting her head on my shoulder.

"Who are you talking about?" she asked.

I hesitated. I usually tried to keep Shannon out of my work-related business, but I was actively working on our relationship and trying to bridge the gap between us. I figured that if I opened up to her a little more about all aspects of my life that she would recognize how important she was to me.

"That nigga Luke," I answered her.

"Which one is that, baby?"

"That's Aaron's right-hand man. He's the one that I'm always bumping heads with," I explained. "I may have to bite the bullet and accept direction from Aaron, but I don't report to Luke."

"It's only temporary," Shannon said in a reassuring tone. "When your dad comes back, everything will go back to normal, right?"

I shrugged my shoulders.

"That's the thing though, Shan. Ain't no telling when Pops is going to be back. Nana's cancer has spread, and I know that he's not going to leave her now," I responded.

"Is Aaron that bad?"

I shrugged my shoulders again.

"I mean … he's smart as hell. There's no way he could be the son of Manny Mercer and not know how to handle business," I told her. "I just don't like anything about how this situation is being handled. Yeah, I may have fucked up by putting that young boy Carlos on, but I took care of that."

I had shared some of the details with Shannon about Carlos's role in past events and his unfortunate demise.

"These niggas waltzed in and took control of everything. I can't even wipe my ass without making sure they're okay with the type of toilet paper that I'm using. I ain't used to that shit. I ain't never had to answer to anyone besides my dad and Deuce," I told her, "but at the end of the day, I'm still getting my money. So, if I'm going to get paid regardless of my contribution, I don't have to be around to deal with their shit. It's not like they're letting me do anything anyway."

"This too shall pass," she said as she kissed me on the cheek. "I'm going to hop in the shower and then we can grab something to eat."

"Cool."

Shannon rolled out of bed and headed for our bathroom. I heard her turn on the shower and my phone started to vibrate again. I checked the phone to see who it was. This time it was Brianna.

"Hello," I answered quietly.

"Hey, you ... am I going to see your face tonight?"

I looked over my shoulder to make sure that Shannon was still in the bathroom before I responded.

"Nah. Not tonight. I got something going on with work," I lied. "I'll try to swing through tomorrow though."

"Is everything okay with work?" she asked.

Brianna had been around for several months, and because of that, I had grown comfortable with her. Way more comfortable than any other side chick I had dealt with. Because she didn't know that she was a side chick, I had to keep up the charade that we were building something substantial. Either way, I had shared details about business with her as well.

"Everything is fine. I just have to meet up with Aaron and Luke about a few changes coming down the pipeline."

Another lie. I had no plans of meeting up with Aaron and Luke that night or the next. If there were any changes or developments, I damn sure wouldn't be the first person to know. Brianna didn't know that though. I still maintained my boss status, as far as she was concerned.

"That's fine. I understand you have to take care of business. Just hit me up tomorrow when you're free," she said.

"For sure. I'll definitely do that," I said.

After a few more moments of small talk, I ended the call with Brianna right before Shannon returned to our bedroom.

"What do you have a taste for?" Shannon asked as she started to get dressed for dinner.

"Whatever you want is cool with me. Let me hop in the shower real quick, and then it's your pick," I said.

Shannon agreed, and I headed into the bathroom. Shannon was attractive, and I was definitely glad that we were on better terms. However, I would be lying if I didn't admit that thoughts of Brianna flooded my mind while I took my shower. I couldn't shake her, and I was determined to find a way to have them both.

JADA

*A*fter spending Christmas Eve in Atlanta with my family, Aaron and I headed to Miami on Christmas morning. It ended up being a lovely day spending time with his immediate and extended family on both the Ramirez and Mercer sides. I also had the opportunity to spend quality time with Olivia, which I appreciated. I was glad that she and I were forming a bond – especially since she had a sibling on the way. A week after taking the home pregnancy test, I was able to make an appointment with my OB/GYN who confirmed the pregnancy. At the time of the appointment, I was already thirteen weeks along and getting ready to start my second trimester. This was a major relief to both the doctor and me since neither of my prior pregnancies survived past nine weeks.

Although things were off to a good start, my doctor still wanted to monitor me closely. She allowed my travel for the time being but advised that I may eventually have to stop traveling back and forth to Miami. In the meantime, I was instructed to take several precautions, including monitoring my stress levels. During the week of Christmas, I reached seventeen weeks into my pregnancy, and we still had not shared the good news with family or friends. Aaron was eager, but I was still hesitant. I wanted a little more time to make sure that everything was fine before I got anyone's hopes up – especially our closest family and friends. I hadn't even told Vanessa, but I knew that with a rapidly growing pudge the cat would soon be out of the bag.

We had one day left in Miami before we returned to Atlanta. While Aaron was still showing me around and getting me comfortable with his hometown, he took me to one of his favorite chicken wing places for a casual lunch. After only eating three of my lemon pepper wings, I was pushing my side salad around my plate with my fork. Aaron was texting on his cell phone, but he looked over at me with concern.

"Is everything okay with your food?" he asked.

I nodded and sat my fork down. My appetite had been very up and down for the last several weeks. Morning sickness and low energy levels were taking a toll on me.

"Everything's fine. I'm just not very hungry at the moment. I might just take the rest to go."

"Are you feeling okay?"

I nodded and smiled. I loved the way he always showed his concern for me, even when he was busy.

"I'm fine. Just a little tired," I answered. "I'll probably lay down for a nap when we get back to the house."

Underneath the table, Aaron rubbed my thigh and leaned over to kiss my cheek. "Alright," he said, "but if something starts to bother you, let me know."

"I will," I assured him as I placed my hand on top of his and gave it a gentle, reassuring squeeze.

Out of the corner of my eye, I could see a woman approaching our table. When Aaron looked up and recognized the woman headed towards us, he mumbled a curse word and released a heavy, frustrated sigh. The short, curvy light-skinned woman was attractive with a face full of makeup and a head full of weave. Her Gucci dress and six-inch heels made me feel very underdressed in the distressed denim shorts and loose racer-back tank top that I wore.

"Hey Aaron," she greeted with a smile and a wink that was all too familiar for my liking.

"What's up Kara?" he asked in an even tone.

"I'm in town for a video shoot. I remembered you telling me about this place, so I decided to stop by and try it out with one of my girls. I figured I would come over and say hello when I spotted you with your ... friend," she said as she cut her eyes towards me.

"My woman," Aaron quickly corrected her.

"Your woman, huh? ... and you're not going to introduce us? How rude," Kara said as she turned towards me and extended her hand. "I'm Kara."

I shook her hand. "Jada. Nice to meet you."

Kara's smile was faker than the twenty-six inches of hair sewn onto her head. "Uh-huh," she said, turning her attention back towards Aaron. "So, this is why you've been avoiding my calls lately?"

This? I thought to myself. I secretly hoped that Aaron checked her before I had to.

"Kara, cut the shit. I ain't in the mood for any of your drama. I haven't been answering your calls because we have nothing to talk about. Whatever you and I had is a thing of the past, and it wasn't even that serious then," Aaron told her.

Kara's eyes widened. "So, this is serious?" she asked in disbelief while she waved a hand in my direction.

I turned towards Aaron. I wasn't sure if I was cranky because of my pregnant hormones, but I had quickly had my fill of Kara. "Babe," I said to him. "That's her last time referring to me as a 'this'."

Aaron rubbed my thigh again. To Kara, he said, "Look I don't know what you even came over here for, but you can leave. Matter of fact, that would probably be in your best interest."

Kara smirked. "I suppose you're right. I don't know why I was so hung up on you anyway. I mean the dick was good, but it wasn't good enough for you to keep dogging me out for this," she said, taking another jab at me.

I shook my head and laughed. Kara was obviously lying in an attempt to save face.

"Bitch don't get fucked up in here," I said in a voice low enough not to attract attention from other diners.

Kara laughed and shook her head. "Wow. I'm surprised at you, Aaron. A man of your stature slumming it with a hood rat is quite surprising," she said. She licked her lips and said, "I always thought you would settle down with a lover, not a fighter."

Aaron pushed away from the table, rising to his feet. "Kara, you ain't the only one that can make a scene, and you know I ain't the one for the bullshit. You're not gonna continue to stand here in my face and disrespect me or my girl."

"Whatever," Kara said as she rolled her eyes and turned to walk away. She mumbled, "I got a new nigga anyway. Ain't nobody worried about you."

Instead of sitting down, Aaron reached into his pocket and pulled out a wad of cash. After dropping tip money onto the table, he grabbed his cell phone and keys before turning towards me.

"You ready to go?"

I nodded and stood up from the table as well. After shouldering my purse, I allowed Aaron to take my hand and steer me out of the restaurant. Before we could reach the truck, someone else approached Aaron.

"What's up, Black?"

The two greeted each other, and I stood to the side quietly while the men engaged in a few moments of small talk. When they were finished speaking, Aaron walked me over to the car where Julio was already holding the door open. Aaron helped me into the truck before getting in on the other side. He waited until Julio pulled away from the restaurant before he spoke.

"I'm sorry about all that shit in there," he said, holding my hand. "That girl is insane. I don't know why I ever messed around with her."

I shrugged my shoulders. "It is what it is. You shut it down. That's all that matters. I can't be upset that you have a past. We all do."

Aaron nodded in acknowledgment of my words.

"I hear what you're saying mama, but I mean ... I can at least try to explain. I hadn't seen her in a few months before the night I met you. She's probably just mad that I'm not interested in her anymore," he explained.

"For real. It's cool. I'm not interested in that part of your past."

"What part are you interested in?"

"Why does everyone down here call you Black?"

Aaron shrugged his shoulders. "It's a little nickname I picked up when I was younger."

"How young and how did it originate?"

"I don't know. I guess when I first started working for my dad," he answered. "I wasn't always the quick-witted problem solver that I am now. My dad wanted to make sure that I could defend myself in any situation, so he had me working with the muscle. He wanted to make sure that there was no fear in the heart of the man that would one day fill his shoes."

He paused and then turned to look in my eyes.

"So, you used to kill people for the Cartel?"

Aaron shrugged his shoulders again. "We all do what we have to do," he said, "and I am pretty good at it. It was said that for any of my marks my face would be the last thing they would see before it all faded to black. Lights out."

"Okay."

"Okay?"

"Yeah," I responded. "You answered my question. Aaron, I know who your family is … who my dad is … who my brother is. I'm not naïve. I know what you are involved in."

He nodded slowly. "Anything else from my past that you want to know about?"

"Isabela," I answered without hesitation.

Aaron sighed.

"I want to know the whole story about your daughter's mother," I told him. "I know that you two are not together, and that you've been raising Olivia for years. There's a story there. It's not often that a single dad has full custody of his daughter."

"She got herself into a bad situation, and I had to step up and do what I needed to do for my child," he answered in a matter of fact tone.

I reached over to rub his shoulder gently. "There's more to that story, baby. She got herself into a bad situation? What does that even mean? How did you two meet? How long were you together? Does she still live in Miami? I want to know the real story."

Aaron's jaw was tight, and he looked out of the window.

"She was one of Regina's friends," he said. "I met her when I was eighteen, and she was twenty. We flirted back and forth for a while but didn't really start dating until about two years later. We had Olivia three years after that."

"How long were you together after Olivia was born?"

"About two years."

"Why did it end?"

Aaron fell silent again. Still looking out of the window he said, "She had jealously and trust issues. She wasn't raised in this lifestyle, and she couldn't handle it. She always thought I was out cheating on her when I was just busy with work. To get back at me she started partying a lot ... and then she started using."

"Using?"

"Drugs. Blow," he said, turning to look at me. "She turned into a coke head. I tried to help her with her addiction. I even put word out on the street that I didn't want anybody selling to her. She got clean for a minute, but then she started fucking some nigga behind my back and got her drugs from him."

"What happened then?" I asked.

Aaron shook his head. "I think you already know what happened to the dude," he said. "As far as Isabela goes, I deaded the relationship. She blamed me for everything. Basically said that it was my fault she turned to another man and drugs, because I wasn't giving her the attention she needed."

"How did you get Olivia?"

Aaron smirked and shook his head again. "Because Isabela said that she never wanted to be a mother in the first place," he answered. "She signed custody over to me, and I sent her ass back to rehab. She pops up every now and then asking to see Olivia or looking for a handout. She is Olivia's mother so I'm never going to leave her high and dry, but she isn't anyone that you ever have to worry about."

I nodded in acknowledgment of his words. "I'm not worried," I told him truthfully. "I just want to know everything about you."

Aaron flashed me his signature half-smile and kissed the back of his hand. "I'm not worried either," he said. "You and Isabela are nothing alike."

AARON

True to her word, Jada headed straight for the room to take a nap when we returned home from lunch. I made sure she was settled, and then I went in search of my father. When I made my way downstairs, I ran into my mother passing through the foyer.

"Hey, Ma," I greeted her with a hug.

"Mi Amor," she said. "What are you up to?"

"Looking for dad. Is he here?" I asked.

She nodded. "He's down the hall in the study," she answered. "Where is Jada?"

"She's upstairs in our room."

"Napping?" my mother asked with a suspicious look.

"Yeah, Ma. She's taking a nap."

"Hmmm," she said with narrowed eyes.

I shook my head and tried to fight off a laugh. My mother was nosy, and I was sure that she would be the first one to notice something different.

"Is she okay? She sure has been doing a lot of sleeping and eating since you guys came into town," she said with a slight smile. "And that beautiful face of hers is getting a little more … round."

"Ma, she's fine."

"You sure there isn't something you want to tell me?" she asked, folding her arms across her chest.

"I don't have anything to tell right now," I responded as I threw my hands up defensively.

"Nothing to tell … right now. Interesting."

"Ma, come on. Stop it," I said as I looked down at the ground and shoved my hands into the pockets of my pants.

I couldn't fight the smile that was pulling at my own lips. My mother nodded in acknowledgment. It was obvious that she had read between the lines and knew what I was not yet able to say. She rubbed my forearm.

"Don't worry. I won't say a word. Just know that when she's ready to tell the good news we will be more than happy to share in your excitement," she said.

"Thanks, Ma."

I kissed her on the cheek and started down the hall to my father's study. I knocked on the door before entering.

"Come in."

I stepped in the room to find my father and my uncle Nate.

"What up, Unc? I greeted him.

"Ain't shit, nephew. Your dad and I came into some information that may be important to you and what's going on in Atlanta," he said.

Nate wasn't my father's blood brother, but they were just as close. They had been friends for as long as anyone could remember. From my understanding, the two of them along with Luke's father – prior to his death – were friends since their teens.

"Yeah, I got my dad's text saying that we needed to talk while I was out with Jada," I responded. "What's going on?"

My dad sighed.

"Do you know of any connection between Julian and the Hit Twins?"

My face wrinkled into a frown.

"The Hit Twins? Mikey and Michaela Pitt?" I asked in confusion. "No. Not really. I don't even know if he's ever had to use them before. He's got a pretty solid crew of hittas on his own team."

"Well, from my understanding, the twins are in Atlanta," my dad said.

"For what?"

"That's what we're trying to figure out," Uncle Nate answered. "Someone else was trying to get in contact with them about a potential job, but they got word that the twins are going to be unavailable for a while. After a little digging around it turns out that they are working on something in Atlanta. It sounds like it might be something personal too."

"Personal? How?" I asked. "They don't even have ties to the south like that. Aren't they from the DMV area?"

Uncle Nate nodded. I continued to speak.

"I thought they didn't even really do business in the south like that. I know they've done a couple of things for us, but I don't know who they would even know in Atlanta," I said.

"That's what we're trying to figure out," Uncle Nate answered. "From my understanding they don't really have any ties to the south. The only person I can think of that they vaguely might know in Atlanta would be Julian."

"That doesn't make any sense," I said out loud.

My dad shrugged his shoulders. "We're trying to make sense of it," he said. "In the meantime, I think you should keep your guard up. I don't want to alarm Julian since he's dealing with his mom's illness, but I want you to make sure that his people in Atlanta are protected. Just in case."

I shrugged my shoulders. "I don't know about this, Pops."

"We're working on getting to the bottom of it, but you need to make sure that the people in Atlanta are on high alert," my dad said. "Regardless of the reason, the Hit Twins are in Atlanta for an unpaid, personal job. If they turned down a paid job for whatever mission they are on right now, you know it's serious."

"I hear you. I can't take it lightly," I agreed. "I'll make sure everyone is being cautious."

"Not just the people that work for him, Black," Uncle Nate said. "If the Pitt Twins are on a personal mission. You need to make sure that you protect Julian's family too."

My father nodded. "I agree. Until we know exactly what's going on you need to make sure that his family is safe ... Jada, Ayanna, and even Cameron."

"Alright," I agreed.

I had no reservations about ensuring the safety of my woman and her sister. However, I knew that protecting Cameron was going to be a challenge. He was careless and quick-tempered which was often a dangerous combination for men in our line of work. If I was lucky, there was someone else in Atlanta that the Hit Twins had a problem with. When Jada and I made it back into town, I was going to make sure that we were prepared for the worst, but I hoped it didn't come to that. Very few people survived with a target on their back from Mikey and Michaela Pitt.

AARON

"*W*hat?" I asked Jada. "In the middle of the day?"

"In the middle of the damn day," she responded. "Tiffany said the cops should be there soon, and I'm on my way there now. I know the team is probably shook up."

I let out a deep breath and shook my head.

"I'm in the middle of something, but I can wrap this up and head that way now."

"I'm fine. The cops should be there shortly. I just wanted to let you know what was going on.".

"Nah, I'm not fine with you being over there by yourself especially with you ..." I stopped speaking when I remembered that I wasn't in the room by myself.

Jada was still pretty adamant about not letting anyone know that she was pregnant. We were past the halfway mark of the pregnancy. I was eager to share the news but wanted to be respectful of her wishes.

"Let me at least get over there and see what it's looking like and how long I'm even going to be there," she said.

"Fine," I answered, "but if you don't call me back in thirty minutes, I'm heading that way."

"Baby, I promise it's okay. There's been a number of burglaries at the boutiques and shops throughout Buckhead. Unfortunately, this isn't anything different, but yes, I'll call you soon," she agreed. "I love you."

"I love you too," I said as I ended the call.

I put the phone back into my pocket. When I turned around, Luke had an expectant look on his face.

"Everything good?" he asked.

I shrugged my shoulders. "Jada's store got robbed."

"The boutique? Is she okay?" PO asked.

I nodded. "Yeah, she's fine. She wasn't there. I just ..." I stopped myself again before sharing my real concern. Jada would kill me if I spilled the beans.

"I'm sure she'll be fine," PO said. "Julian's been taking the girls to the shooting range for a long time, and Jada's actually pretty nice with a handgun. The bad guys won't want to see her."

PO laughed to lighten the mood. I just wanted to finish our business so I could check on her.

Almost as if he were reading my mind Luke said, "Let's wrap this up so you can go check on your girl, man."

"Alright," I said, sitting back down in my chair. "We upped the muscle and streamlined the process for money and product handoffs, but if there are any other precautions you can think of let's make sure we do that too. It's been a couple of weeks. We haven't seen anything too out of the ordinary, but if the Pitt Twins are in Atlanta, I don't want to take any chances."

PO shrugged his shoulders. "I think you're doing all that you can, man. Short of making sure the girls have security every-where they go, you're making sure that everyone is on guard and alert."

"I thought about sticking Jada and Ayanna with security, but I'm trying not to overreact," I said. "We haven't heard any noise from the twins, and I'm not trying to freak them out. Jada and

Ayanna don't really know what's going on. I'm trying not to bring them into the middle of this."

Luke narrowed his eyes while he sat in silence.

"Black, what's the twins' names again?" he asked.

"Mikey and Michaela Pitt."

Luke let out a deep sigh and shook his head. "Initials MP ... like MP1 and MP2?"

Shit, I thought to myself as PO and I both let out heavy sighs. If the MPs working with Carlos were in fact Mikey and Michaela Pitt, then we had a serious problem on our hands. They were highly skilled assassins that moved meticulously. Julian Reid's organization had been having problems for months. If the Pitt Twins were behind it, there was no telling how much inside information they really had on our team. Without knowing what their end game was, there was no way I could stay two steps ahead of them. When my father and Uncle Nate informed me of their suspicions, I didn't want to alarm Jada without having anything confirmed. The last thing I wanted was to cause her unnecessary stress.

Knowing that Mikey and Michaela Pitt were probably the culprits behind the chaos I was battling changed everything – especially since their mission was personal. They had already affected our pockets. I was not going to allow them to affect the family too.

"Carlos had numbers in his phone," PO said. "Did anything ever come from that?"

Luke shook his head. "Nah, man. The numbers were disconnected when I tried to follow up. They were unregistered burner phones. There wasn't any information to be traced."

"The phones went dead after Cameron took Carlos out," I said. "How would they even know what happened?"

PO shrugged his shoulders again. "Your guess is as good as mine. I assume they knew what was up when they couldn't get in contact with him anymore."

"Or they have another man inside," I mumbled.

"I'm gonna call Unc and see about getting some more muscle up here from Miami," Luke said, referring to my Uncle Nate. "We can't afford to get caught slipping, because we waited until it was too late to take action. PO and I will take care of everything here. Go on and check on your girl."

I stood up and reached for my keys when Luke spoke again.

"Black, I know you don't want Jada in the middle of your business, but she's your blind spot right now," he said. "Make sure that she's taken care of so you can take care of business without any distraction."

I nodded and said my goodbyes before heading out of the house.

CAMERON

I lit my blunt and raised it to my lips while I sat alone in the basement of the meeting house. Aaron and Luke called a brief meeting that afternoon, and I had arrived early. Being back home with Shannon was nice, but she was all up under me. If I wasn't working, I was with her. That left little time for Brianna. I figured if I got to the house ahead of the meeting then she could stop by for a moment before Aaron and his goons showed up. Truth be told, I had no idea what the meeting was about. I didn't care either. I found it quite entertaining that he removed me from a seat of power and still hadn't been able to find a way to get things under control.

It was the beginning of February, and we had been having problems with rival dealers new to the area, infighting amongst our team, and money coming up short. The whole time my father was concerned about me not being able to handle business it actually turned out that Manny Mercer and his son couldn't do it either. There was no doubt that we were still in control of Atlanta. I didn't see that changing anytime soon, but nothing was going smoothly. In all the years that I worked with my dad, I never saw the number of problems that we faced with KS9 and whatever forces we were currently battling.

I was halfway finished with my blunt when Brianna sent a text letting me know that she was outside. I jogged up the stairs to let her in through the front door.

"Hey, you," she said, kissing me on the lips.

"Hey," I greeted her quickly and let her into the house.

Before closing the door, I looked up and down the street to make sure that I didn't see any other cars I recognized. I wanted to make sure that no one else saw her entering the house. The last thing I needed was for someone who knew Shannon to go running their mouth to her. Before I could even lock the door, Brianna was all over me.

"Slow down, baby," I joked. "We got a little time."

"I just missed you," she said into my ear while fumbling with my belt. "I haven't seen you in over a week."

"I know. I've been busy."

That wasn't really a lie. Aaron hadn't really told me exactly was going on, but he started including me in more of the day to day business. Until things calmed down it was all hands on deck. He and Luke had even arranged to have extra shooters brought up from Miami to make sure that our security was increased. Whether it was picking up money or dropping off drugs, no one in the crew moved without extra security.

"I know you have, but why did I have to meet you over here?" she asked between kisses as she slipped out of her coat. "You never have me over your place anymore."

I sighed. When I left the house that Shannon and I shared, I stayed at Deuce's old house. It was paid off, and neither my father nor I had thought to sell it. Having Deuce's house had come in handy, because I had a place to lay my head away from Shannon and her drama. It also provided me a place to meet up with Brianna. Now that I was back home with Shannon full time, I was having to come up with creative ways to meet up with Brianna. I knew I was taking a risk by having her meet me at the meeting spot, especially when there was a meeting scheduled. I just had to see her. Even though Shannon made me happy, I couldn't bring myself to kick Brianna to the curb.

"I've been busy, Bri. I don't even be at the house like that," I told her.

"But Cam, what is this place?" she asked.

"Come on, man. What's up with all the talking? Did you come over here to play twenty questions?" I asked her.

Brianna shook her head. "No. I didn't come over here to talk at all," she said as she dropped her purse by the door.

"Exactly," I said. "Come on."

I led her towards one of the back bedrooms. The room was simple. Honestly, most of the house was simple, but it served its purpose. No one lived there anyway. Occasionally some of the crew would work late into the night and would eventually crash at the house, but that didn't happen often. As Brianna pulled off her sweater, I thought about how Shannon wouldn't be caught dead having sex in a glorified trap house. The two women were so different from one another, but I needed them both in my life.

I ended up getting so caught up with Brianna that I lost track of time. Before I knew it, I heard keys turning in the lock of the front door while Brianna and I were rushing to put our clothes back on.

"How long are you going to be over here today?" she asked.

I shrugged my shoulders in response. I shook my head when I heard Luke's voice in the hallway. He was speaking on the phone.

"I don't know, but I'll hit you up later," I told Brianna as I walked towards the door.

I had paused with my hand on the doorknob when I heard Luke speak again.

"Yeah, he's already here. Got some bitch with him too," Luke told whoever he was speaking too. "She left her purse and her coat by the front door. You need to tell your boy this ain't no goddamn motel."

"Some bitch?" Brianna questioned with a frown on her face.

She wasn't the only one that didn't take kindly to Luke's conversation. I opened the bedroom door and started down the hallway with Brianna close on my heels.

"Alright, man. You can handle that. I'll see you when you get here," Luke ended his call and made direct eye contact with me.

Brianna shot Luke a dirty look while she reached to pick up her coat and her purse. Luke ignored her, keeping his attention focused on me.

"I'd walk your company on out, if I were you," he said.

Before his statement, I had every intention of walking Brianna out the front door. However, Luke's instruction and demeanor caused me to change my plan.

"But you're not me," I told him, "and if I were you, I'd mind my own business."

Luke shook his head and laughed. "Yeah, alright."

Before either of us could say anything else, the door opened and few other crewmembers walked in. A couple of them gave Brianna a questioning look, but none of them said a word. I took Brianna's hand and led her down to the basement. In the back of my mind, I knew that she had no business being in the house – let alone the basement – but Luke needed to know that he didn't run shit. I was sure that Luke had been on the phone with Aaron moments earlier. If Aaron had an issue with my company, then he would have to be the one to say something to me. I was tired of all the middleman shit with his homeboy.

. . .

AARON

In the time since Luke, PO, and I determined that the two MPs were the Pitt Twins, the three of us made the necessary changes behind the scenes to step security up further. Due to the disturbances we were still had, I was hesitant to let the whole team know what was going on. I was convinced that Mikey and Michaela still had an inside man. However, if the twins were still coming after associates of the Reid organization, both professionally and personally, it was only fair to let the rest of the guys know what we were up against. I was meeting with the more senior members of the crew and some of the muscle.

When I pulled up to the house, I recognized all but one of the cars present. I had hoped that Cameron's female friend was gone. With everything going on, the last thing I wanted was to go back and forth with him. He had been a royal pain in my ass since I got to Atlanta. There was no more patience for him. I thought I had made that clear when he had been demoted before Thanksgiving. I was trying to keep things at a respectful level because of his last name.

I parked and quickly entered the house. I did not intend for the meeting to last long. I still had to talk to Jada about the increased security I required her to have. I knew she wouldn't be happy about it, and I was saving my energy for that conversation. I headed down to the basement, pushing open the door that was already cracked. Blue was the first person to greet me.

"What's up, man?" Blue asked as we slapped hands.

"Man, you wouldn't believe me if I told you," I answered, shaking my head.

The room was pretty full as there should have been about twenty men in attendance. As I stepped further into the basement, I shook my head again at the sight before me. Cameron sat at a table in the corner, oblivious to my presence while he smoked a blunt. Not only had he invited Dre, who I still didn't trust, but he also had some woman in his lap that I was unfamiliar with. That was not the way that I conducted business. Cameron looked up from his company to see me standing in the middle of the room. He motioned for me to come towards where he was sitting, but I declined. Cameron smirked and shook his head.

"What's up, man?" Cameron questioned. "What's so important that you called us all down here?"

"No disrespect, but I don't know your company. I don't discuss business in front of people I don't know."

We exchanged hard stares as the room started to quiet. The tension between Cameron and I had been building for months and could easily be felt throughout the basement.

"So, you want me to put my company out?" Cameron asked with a laugh.

I shrugged my shoulders. "You can leave with her. It's all the same to me," I answered.

Cameron's female friend looked at him with a frown, but he kept his frown directed at me.

"Cam, are seriously going to let this nigga put me out?" she asked in disbelief.

A few of the men in the room looked on with widened eyes at the disrespect of her referring to me as 'this nigga'. She obviously had no idea who I was.

Cameron gently patted her thigh and looked into her eyes. "Why don't you head upstairs for a little bit? I won't be down here long."

Cameron's female companion rolled her neck and sucked her teeth. "Are you fucking kidding me right now?" she mumbled as she stood up from Cameron's lap.

When he didn't respond she stormed out of the room, bumping into me in the process. After she slammed the door, Cameron stood up from his chair.

"Alright, man. What the fuck is going on?" Cameron asked.

"I need to bring everyone up to speed on what's going on," I said. "I don't know how many of you all are familiar with the Pitt twins."

Cameron frowned. "The brother and sister contract killers from DC? The Hit Twins?"

"Yeah, man. The Hit Twins."

Cameron shrugged his shoulders and stuck his hands into his pockets. "I know that they're no joke. If they're after you, you're pretty much a goner ... but why are we talking about them?"

"Because they're in Atlanta and word on the street is that they're after your family," I answered. "They're probably the forces behind the issues we've been dealing with for months."

Some of the men throughout the room shook their heads in disbelief. They knew who the Pitt twins were and what they were all about.

"Word on the street, huh?" Cameron asked, sounding unconvinced. "Why in the hell would they be after us?"

I shrugged my shoulders. "That's what Luke and I have been trying to figure out."

Cameron shook his head and rolled his eyes. "Who put out a hit?"

"My pops has his ear to the streets, but it doesn't sound like a paid hit," I explained. "Whatever they're doing, it's personal. They're coming for anyone and anything associated with the Reid last name."

Cameron laughed and shook his head again. "Yeah okay."

My jaw tightened at Cameron's dismissive behavior. I wasn't in the mood for his shit. Luke stepped up and addressed Cameron before I could.

"Look, man, we're already doing all we can to protect the business. Your father and your grandmother are safe where they are. We're going to make sure that your sisters are straight," Luke said, "but you and everyone else here may want to make sure that you stay on alert, especially now that you all know why we've been taking extra precautionary measures. Cameron, you're the one with the Reid last name. You should definitely beef up your own personal security."

Cameron laughed a little harder in the otherwise quiet room. "Seriously?" he asked. "You want me to up my muscle because Aaron and his dad are overreacting to some street rumor?"

I shook my head. "Cameron, I think you're underestimating the information that my father and I have access to," I told him. "I don't think the suspicious activity around here is just a coincidence. I don't think the robbery at Jada's store was a coincidence. The Hit twins could be coming for anybody with the Reid last name. Your sisters are not an exception. Like Luke just said, we're going to make sure that your sisters are fine. If you don't want to take any extra measure for yourself, that's on you."

"I don't need any advice from either one of you on how to take care of my family. Before you two showed up, I was doing that for years," Cameron stated with narrowed eyes.

"I'm sure you did a mighty fine job when your brother and your father were around, but neither of them are here and you haven't necessarily been pulling your own weight," I said to him. "Even when your father and Deuce were here, you never had to go against the Hit Twins."

"I'm pretty sure I'll be just fine. You two can handle the business, but I can handle taking care of my family. Just because you've been messing around with my sister doesn't mean that she's your concern. I've got Jada. That's my blood," Cameron stated with a clenched jaw.

"And she's carrying my blood. So, I will worry about her. Always."

Cameron had pissed me off to the point where the words had come out of my mouth before I could stop myself. We stared at each other while the other men in the room fell completely silent. Everyone realized that I had just admitted Jada's pregnancy, and all eyes were on Cameron while he stared at me with a clenched jaw. I shook my head and released a deep, frustrated sigh.

Jada was going to kill me.

JADA

I hadn't seen Vanessa in months. We were both so busy during the holiday season, and then she accompanied DJ on another tour. Time had passed so quickly that we had not seen each other since the day of the salon's grand opening – which was also the day I found out I was pregnant. Needless to say, Vanessa had not been an exception to my decision to keep the pregnancy quiet. It was not the sort of thing that I had wanted to share over the phone. Fresh off the tour, DJ and Vanessa were back in town, and she called to invite me to lunch. Unsure of what I wanted to eat, I suggested she meet me at my condo so we could catch up and decide on what food to have delivered.

I was relaxing on my bed waiting for the front desk to alert me of Vanessa's arrival, when she knocked on my front door. I made my way to the front door to let her in.

"Front desk still letting you right up, huh?" I greeted her with a smile.

"You know it," she laughed as she walked into my place.

Vanessa walked into the living room and sat her purse and coat down on the couch while I closed the front door. She turned to face me as I joined her in the living room. She looked me up and down with narrowed, suspicious eyes.

"You look very ... casual," she said.

I looked down at the loose sweater dress I was wearing. "Is that a compliment?" I asked.

"Yes ... but you just don't normally where your clothes that loose, Jada," Vanessa said. "I can see it all in your face. Is there something you need to tell me?"

I started laughing, and I shrugged my shoulders. "Yeah. I didn't think it was something I should tell you over the phone."

"Oh my goodness!" Vanessa squealed as she rushed to hug me. "Aw, Jay. I'm so happy for you. Both of you! This is awesome. How far along are you?"

"Five months," I answered.

"Come on. Let's sit down," Vanessa said in an excited tone. "Tell me everything! How did you find out? What did Aaron say? How are you feeling so far? What are your doctors saying?"

Vanessa and I caught up on the information surrounding my pregnancy. I told her she was the first person to find out and why I had been keeping it a secret. Having been for both of my miscarriages, she understood why I hesitated to share the news, but she was very excited that everything was going well so far. We were deciding on what to eat when my cell phone rang.

"Is pizza okay?" Vanessa asked. "Has the baby been giving you heartburn?"

I shook my head. "Just a little bit, but not enough to turn down pizza," I laughed. I reached for my cell phone and saw that Cameron was calling me. "It's Cameron. Let me get this."

I touched the screen to answer the call, but before I could greet my brother, he started speaking.

"So, I hear congratulations are in order ... again."

I frowned because the tone of his voice was anything but congratulatory. Instead, it was angry and harsh.

"Excuse me?"

"Dammit, Jada! You didn't waste any time, huh?" Cameron spat.

"Whoa! What is wrong with you?"

"I could ask you the same thing, sis. Was the situation with Israel not painful enough for you?" he asked. "Did you have to go and put yourself in the exact same situation?"

"First of all, Cameron Jermaine Reid, I don't know who the hell you think you're talking to but you need to watch your tone of voice," I snapped at him. "Second, don't you ever compare Israel and Aaron. It is not the same –"

"Don't kid yourself, Jada. It's the exact same situation. You got yourself knocked up by another nigga that's going to leave you!"

I bit the inside of my cheek to keep the tears from spilling onto my cheeks that were flushed red with anger. Out of the corner of my eye, I saw Vanessa looking at me with concern.

"I mean seriously, Jada. He's obviously been enjoying himself during his extending visit to the A, but what are you going to do when he up and goes back to Miami? Huh? His family, his business, his whole life is in Miami."

I was silent as I continued to hold the phone up to my ear. I stood up from the couch walking over to the wall of windows in the living room, my back towards Vanessa and my front door.

"You didn't think about that, did you?" Cameron's voice broke into my thoughts.

"I'm not doing this with you," I stated evenly as I furiously wiped away a tear from the corner of my eye.

Behind me, I heard the key turn in the lock before the front door opened and closed. I was livid. I heard footsteps behind me as Aaron walked to where I was standing. Without turning to face him, I knew that he was right behind me.

Ignoring my previous statement Cameron continued to speak. "I bet you didn't think about Mom either, huh?"

"Cameron ..."

I had intended for my voice to come out firm and stern. However, it was barely above a whisper.

"All the private school education, debutante balls, Jack & Jill, and all the other clubs and shit she had you involved in ..." Cameron said. "She spent so much time, energy, and money to separate you from the life that we were born into. She wanted something different for you, and what did you do? You turned around and made yourself some drug dealer's baby mama. What would she think if she could see you now?"

It took all of my strength not to break down and cry. After a brief moment, I gripped my phone tightly and said, "Fuck you, Cameron! I don't know what's been going on with you lately, but you need to get your shit together. If you have a problem with me or my child's father, then you address that. Don't you dare bring mom into it! Don't let her name come out of your mouth to me. Matter of fact, don't speak to me period until you can act like you got some goddamn sense!"

I ended the call before he could say anything else to me. Aaron placed a hand on my shoulder, but I pulled away and turned around to face him. Aaron's facial expression dropped when he saw how visibly upset I was.

"You told Cameron?"

Aaron sighed and tried to reach for my hand. I snatched away from him. Vanessa stood up from the couch.

"Hey, girl ... I'm going to go home and unpack so you two can talk," she said.

I walked towards Vanessa, leaving Aaron by the windows.

"No, you don't have to leave. I don't have shit to say to him right now," I said. "We can go out for lunch."

I started to gather my things – reaching for my purse and my keys. Vanessa pulled me into a hug and quietly spoke into my ear.

"Jada, don't leave like this. You and I can catch up later. You need to talk to your man."

Vanessa pulled away from our hug and put a cheerful smile on her face.

"I'll catch you two later," she said.

Without protesting, I stood by the sofa and watched as Vanessa get her belongings and let herself out. After a few moments of silence between us, I turned around to face Aaron. He took a couple of steps in my direction, but I took a step backwards.

"Did you tell Cameron?"

Aaron took another step towards me.

"Jay ... it just kind of came out," he answered.

My face twisted into a frown. "How the hell does something like that just *kind of* come out?" I asked angrily. "How do you accidentally tell my brother that I'm pregnant, Aaron?"

Aaron shrugged his shoulders. "There's no excuse. I'm sorry."

"Are you?" I snapped. He frowned at me. "Are you really sorry, Aaron? Or was this just another thing for you to hold over my brother's head in the never-ending power struggle you two are having? Did you finally win the pissing contest?"

"Baby, I –"

"I'm so sick of this shit! I'm tired of being in the middle of y'all bullshit. For most of my life, Cameron has been one of the closest people to me, and I can't believe the way he just spoke to me. All because you're running the business?" I asked. "Our families have been working together for years! Your dad and my dad have been friends for years! Hell, our mothers grew up together! What is the damn problem?"

I didn't realize how upset I was until I could no longer hold back the tears that were spilling onto my face.

"Dammit!" I shouted.

I threw a throw pillow from the couch across the room in

frustration with one hand while my other hand rubbed my swollen belly. Aaron stepped closer to me and took me by my arms, pulling my body closer to him.

"You need to calm down," he said firmly as he pulled me into a hug and rubbed my back. He kissed the top of my head before I hesitantly wrapped my arms around him. "I'm sorry. I didn't mean for it to come out, but I don't know what your brother's problem is either. He's been fighting me every step of the way since I got to Atlanta. Because of his issues, he probably won't be on board with our relationship ... but Jada, this isn't about him. This child ... the future that we're building ... it's about us. If Cameron can't be happy about his new niece or nephew, then that's his problem. He shouldn't be the source of any extra stress for you during this time. If he can't speak to you in a respectful manner, then he doesn't need to speak to you. Period."

I nodded as I pulled away from our embrace.

"I'm sorry too ... for making you keep all of this a secret. Cameron should have already known," I responded. "We're more than halfway through this. I should have already told our family and friends."

"I understand why you didn't," he said. "You were nervous and scared. We're out of the woods though, mama. It's my job to make sure that you don't have anything else to be worried about. I'm right here making sure that everything is going to be okay. Do you trust me?"

"Yes. Of course, I do."

"Good," Aaron said, "because there are some changes that need to take place, and I need you to trust me and follow my lead on this."

"Changes like what?" I asked with narrowed eyes.

"Changes to security and how you make moves when you're not with me."

"What?"

Without answering my question, Aaron looked down at his watch. "Have you eaten lunch yet?"

I shook my head.

"Alright. Grab your stuff and come on," he said. "I'll explain over food."

CAMERON

"You gotta work all night?" Shannon asked.

I leaned against my car and held my phone up to my ear. I checked the time on my watch and saw it was a little before eight o'clock. I was actually almost finished with work, but I had plans to make a detour before heading home.

"I don't know right now," I answered. "It's been a busy week. I might be here for a while, but I'll let you know when I'm on my way home."

"Okay that's fine," Shannon responded. "I'll probably get in the bed after I eat something, but I'll see you when you get here. Love you."

"Love you too," I said before ending the call.

I pulled the phone away from my ear, but instead of sliding it back into my pocket, I sent a text to Brianna telling her that I would be headed to her place as soon as things wrapped up. I was hopeful we'd be finished within the next few minutes or so. Luke and PO were tied up with other business-related activities, so I was waiting for one of our dealers to pick up their product for the week. Due to the issues we encountered over the previous months, we had changed the pickup location from the tire warehouse to the abandoned facility in the old industrial complex that my father used the previous year. Ordinarily, this would have been something I would have felt comfortable handling by myself, but I was strictly prohibited from doing so because of the alleged threat from the Pitt twins. Instead of hanging out solo, I was waiting around with Dre, Blue, and one of the hired guns from Miami. I rolled my eyes when I thought about the hoops that Aaron Mercer made me jump through.

In the week since Aaron told me about the Pitt Twins and Jada's pregnancy, I had barely spoken to him or my sister. Whenever Aaron and I spoke, the conversations were very brief and only about business. I preferred it that way anyhow. I had not spoken to Jada since the day I found out she was pregnant. Jada had broken the news to our family and her friends, and from my understanding, she and Aaron were in Miami sharing the information with the Mercers. They could shower the parents-to-be with love for their new bundle of joy if they wanted to. I wasn't jumping on that bandwagon.

I heard the door open behind me.

"Aye, man, he still not here yet?" Blue asked in a frustrated tone.

I turned around to face him and shook my head. "Nah, man. He was supposed to be here thirty minutes ago," I answered.

"Bruh, I got somewhere I go," Blue said. "He needs to come the hell on. Shit!"

I nodded in agreement. I turned my attention back towards the parking lot when I heard a vehicle pulling into the lot. I was expecting a silver Chevy sedan but instead Blue and I looked on while a blacked-out Ford truck slowly crept towards us.

"Who the fuck is that?" Blue asked.

We both reached for our weapons.

"I don't know," I said, taking the safety off of my gun.

The car came to a stop a few yards away from me, but the

engine didn't turn off. Blue walked up beside me. Both the driver and passenger side rear doors of the truck opened. Two unfamiliar men hopped out and approached us.

"Can I help you?" Blue asked with a mean glare.

"Yeah. We're looking for Cam," the shorter of the two men responded.

"Who is we?" I asked. "I don't know y'all."

The taller one laughed before saying, "Chill, bruh. Rock sent us to pick up his shit."

Blue shook his head. "Nah. That ain't how this works, and Rock should know better than that," he said. "I ain't handing off shit to somebody I don't know."

The shorter man shook his head and said, "You must be Blue. Yeah, I heard you were a tough guy."

"I don't give a fuck what you heard," Blue commented. "I said what I said. I don't know you, so you can get the hell on."

The taller guy pulled his gun from his waistband.

"You two can sit here going back and forth if you want, but I don't have time for this shit," he said, taking another step in our direction. "I ain't leaving empty handed."

I frowned at the two men standing in front of me. "I don't know who the fuck you think you're talking to, but you not going to be told again that you ain't getting shit. If Rock wants to come back tomorrow, tell him to hit me up, but y'all can get the fuck outta here."

The door to the warehouse opened again. Dre and the Miami muscle joined us outside right as Blue pushed the tall guy with the gun. Pushing and shoving on both ends turned to guns being drawn and punches being thrown. I don't know who fired the first shot, but I did not hesitate to shoot as well. With bullets flying from both directions, it was hard to tell who fired which shots. All I knew was that one of them fired two shots into Blue and took off running as soon as his body hit the ground. As soon as the two hopped into the truck, they peeled out of parking lot quickly.

Dre and the Miami hired gun tried to run after the truck, firing shots at the vehicle as they sped away. When they made it back towards me, I was shaking my head in disbelief while I knelt beside Blue's body.

"Man, what the fuck was that?" the Miami help asked.

"I don't know," I said, shaking my head, "I don't know."

Dre pulled out his phone and looked down at Blue's body. "I'm calling help."

"Do that and stay with him. I'll hit you up later," I said. "Something ain't right. Rock would have never pulled no shit like that. I need to go see about him real quick."

I pulled out my phone and placed a call to Rock. When he didn't answer, I grabbed my keys out of my pocket and hopped into my car. I was headed straight to his spot to figure out what the hell was going on. I shook my head and let out a frustrated sigh as I sped out of the parking lot. I knew that it was going to be a while before I saw either Shannon or Brianna.

JADA

I was really starting to like Miami. Atlanta would always be my home, but the more time I spent in Miami, the more I felt at ease. It also helped matters that the Mercers were accepting me as one of their own – for the most part anyway. Everyone except for Regina was excited when Aaron and I shared the news of the new baby. We were in the middle of a visit to Miami that was scheduled to last the better part of a week. I was quickly approaching the six-month mark of my pregnancy, and the period when my doctor had strongly advised that I cease air travel. This would be my last trip to Miami until the baby was born.

I pulled my legs underneath me and shifted on the patio

sofa. I ran a hand over my growing baby bump and took in my view of the sun setting before me. We had chosen the perfect time to relay the news to his family as I was sure I would not be able to hide my bump any longer. It felt like my stomach was growing more and more every day. While Aaron was off with his father, presumably tending to business, I spent the evening with the Mercer ladies – Sophia, Daniella, Olivia, and Regina. Even with Regina's presence, my time with the ladies was relaxing and refreshing.

Over the past week, Aaron steadily increased security inside and outside of our home. He vaguely expressed that recent events with the business required us to be more careful in our day-to-day lives. Unimpressed with the security of my condo building, he pretty much moved me in with him. I didn't mind, because I spent the majority of my time at his house anyway. The only frustrating thing was that I was not as free to go out and about as I had been previously. If I wasn't with Aaron, he had not allowed me to leave the house without at least one bodyguard. I found it annoying and extreme that I couldn't even go to work without someone breathing down my neck. However, Aaron said that it was not up for discussion. Luckily for me, he knew we didn't have worry about safety within his parents' home.

Olivia excused herself from the veranda to play in her room, and Daniella was off preparing for a date. I took a sip from my glass of water while Sophia and Regina sat on the sofa opposite of me enjoying glasses of wine.

"So, Aaron mentioned you two are having a house built nearby," Sophia said with a wide smile on her face. "Is that true?"

I took another sip of my water and nodded. "Yeah. I'm not selling my place in Atlanta or anything so I imagine there will be a lot of back and forth. Aaron talked about building a home for our family, but I'm sure it will take some time. He's very particular, and he likes expensive things. I wouldn't imagine our house being finished anytime soon."

"So, you will still be staying here with us after the baby is born, yes?" Sophia asked.

"Definitely. Until the house is done, I don't see a need to live anywhere else," I answered. "There's plenty of space here. I wouldn't want to move Olivia from the only home she's ever known until we have something more permanent."

Sofia's smile widened as she clasped her hands together in excitement. "Ah, that's wonderful news. We would love to have you in our home," she said. She turned towards Regina. "Isn't that so wonderful, mija?"

Regina nodded slightly but didn't smile. It would have been obvious to anyone except Sophia that Regina did not share her mother's excitement.

"Oh, Jada! A new house won't be ready for several months. You must let me prepare a nursery for the baby here," she said. "Please. It would give me such joy."

"Sure," I responded with a smile. "That would be nice. Aaron hasn't wanted me to lift a finger lately. He's not thrilled that I'm still working. He would appreciate you taking something like that off of my hands."

"Wonderful! I was hoping you would say that. I suspected you were with child around Christmas but promised not to say anything. I've seen some nursery ideas in a magazine. I want to make sure you love it," she said as she stood up from her seat. "Let me go find it. I'll be right back."

Sophia strolled away from us, leaving the veranda and entering back into the house. Regina hesitated for a moment but also stood up and started towards the door. I called her name before she was able to leave.

"Regina, wait!"

Regina stopped and slowly turned around to face me. I sat my glass on the accent table and rose to my feet. I walked towards her until there was only a foot or so of distance between us. She raised her eyebrows expectantly.

"What's the deal?" I asked. "What is your issue with me?"

Regina ran her fingers through her hair, sweeping it over her shoulder, and her forehead wrinkled into a frown.

"Jada, what are you talking about?"

"I'm trying to understand the cause of the tension between us. There's an uneasiness between us that everyone is aware of except for your mother," I answered. "You've been cold and distant since we met. Have I offended you in some way?"

"I am civil to you," she responded. "What more do you want from me? I have enough friends."

"I'm not looking to be one of your friends, but we are going to be family, Regina," I said to her.

She smirked in response. "We'll see about that."

"Excuse me?" I asked with wide eyes.

"Sweetie, my brother hasn't officially made you a part of this family yet. Just because you're having his child doesn't mean that you will ever have the Mercer last name. Aaron hasn't had the best track record when it comes to picking his significant others," she said. "I don't know what you did to make him so careless that he knocked you up so quickly, but I assure you that won't guarantee a marriage. We'll see how long this thing between the two of you lasts when he sees what I see and realizes how selfish you are. A man like my brother needs someone like our mom. He needs a woman that will be there to support him without question while she takes care of home. He needs someone who understands that the relationship is not a democracy, honey. He's the boss."

I was speechless. Regina continued to speak.

"From what I've seen you're the exact opposite. You are more like Isabela than he realizes. You don't appear to be thrilled about the child that you are carrying – a potential heir to the Mercer empire. Hell, you hid your pregnancy from our family for almost six months. You seem to be more concerned with your friends, your businesses, your life in Atlanta," she commented. "So, like I said ... we'll see if you two love birds actually make it down the aisle."

Still lost for words, eyes still wide, I just stood there glaring at Regina unable to form a response. As much as I wanted to call her the bitch that she had been to me since the day we met, I knew that I wouldn't dare to do so in her family's home. The door opened behind Regina and Sophia made her way back onto the veranda – a smile on her face as she flipped through the pages of some magazine. Once again, she was oblivious to the tension between me and her oldest child.

"Mama, I have to go. I told Diego that I would be home before the girls went to bed," Regina said. "I will call you later."

"Of course. Kiss my babies for me," Sophia responded, kissing Regina on the cheek before taking a seat.

Regina did not even look my way when she left. I rolled my eyes and joined Sophia on the sofa. I spent the next hour or so looking over nursery themes and ideas.

When I made it up to the room, I tried to call Vanessa to tell her about my exchange with Regina, but she didn't answer. I dressed for bed and curled up to watch a Netflix movie, but I was asleep before the opening credits finished. A few hours later I heard Aaron come into the room, even though he tried to move around quietly. He stripped down to his underwear and climbed in bed next to me. His chest was against my back while I laid my side. He rubbed my stomach and kissed my cheek.

"You asleep?" he whispered.

I shook my head and rolled in the direction to face him.

"How was your day?"

He shrugged his shoulders. "It was a day," he said, "but it's better now that I'm with you. Some shit came up with your brother though. We have to go back to Atlanta tomorrow. Our flight leaves in the afternoon."

I released a relieved sigh before I could stop myself. With the light from the TV providing illumination in the otherwise dark room, I could see him raise a suspicious eyebrow at my reaction.

"How was your day?" he asked. "My mother didn't drive you crazy with a bunch of baby stuff, did she?"

I shook my head. "Not at all. We talked about the nursery, but it was nice to see how excited she is."

"So, my mom didn't get on your nerves?"

"No."

He let out a heavy sigh before he asked, "What did Gigi do now?"

I shrugged my shoulders but didn't answer. He already appeared to be tired and stressed from his day. He and my brother were barely on speaking terms so whatever happened that forced us to go back to Atlanta early could not have been good. With Regina's accusations of me being selfish ringing in my ears, I didn't want to bother him with details of my exchange with his sister.

"Jada, what did Gigi say to you?"

"It's not that important," I said, kissing his lips. "I don't want any drama with your sister."

Aaron looked at me expectantly. He wanted an answer to his question.

"Fine," I said. "She doesn't think that our relationship is going to last. She implied that I am just another in the long line of wrong women that you have chosen. She said that I am more like Isabela than you realize and that just because we are having a child doesn't mean that we will have a life together. She thinks I'm temporary."

Aaron sat up in the bed. As he stared straight ahead into the darkness of the room, I could see that his jaw clenched tightly. He was pissed. I sat up as well, rubbing his shoulder reassuringly.

"Babe, I said that I didn't want any drama."

"Gigi needs to keep her fucking mouth shut," he snapped. He relaxed slightly and turned to look at me. "Jada, I knew you were special before you got pregnant. I had already decided that you were the one. I want to spend the rest of my life with you, so fuck all that shit Regina said. You know that what we have is real, and we didn't need ten years to figure that shit out."

"I'm sorry," I said quietly. "I won't mention Regina again."

Aaron sighed and reached for my hand, taking it and kissing it. "You don't have anything to be sorry about. You can talk to me about anything, mama," he said. "I'm just tired of going back and forth with family members about our relationship. I got too much shit on my plate right now to be concerned about the thoughts of your brother or my sister."

"I understand."

Aaron let go of my hand and pushed the covers back on the bed. When he got out of the bed, he pulled on a T-shirt and reached for his cell phone.

"Where are you going?" I asked.

"I need to make a phone call," he answered.

"Can your call wait? Babe, it's almost one o'clock in the morning," I said to him.

"Not everywhere," he responded. He leaned over to kiss me on the forehead. "I might be awhile. Why don't you try to go back to sleep? I'll see you in the morning."

Before I could protest any further, Aaron headed for the balcony, leaving me alone in our bed. This was exactly what I wanted to avoid. He already had enough on his mind without my issues with his sister. Frustrated by our conversation, I turned on my side and closed my eyes.

AARON

I stepped onto the balcony and closed the door. I had not felt this level of stress in years. Again, I questioned my decision to go to Atlanta in the first place, but I stopped myself. If I had never gone to Atlanta, I would not have to deal with the shit show that the Reid organization had turned into. On the other hand, I never would have met Jada. That was one of the few things I did not want to change. I could not imagine my life without the younger daughter of Julian Reid. Despite whatever Cameron thought and the words that Regina said to her, Jada was not temporary. She and everyone else needed to know that.

I scrolled through the contacts in my phone until I landed on the person I intended to reach. I touched the screen to initiate the call and held the phone up to my ear. A few moments later, the call was answered.

"Aaron, what's up?" Julian asked on the other end of the call.

I sighed. "A lot, man ... a lot," I answered truthfully. "How's your mom doing?"

"Not well," Julian answered. "My sisters know, but I haven't told my kids yet. She probably doesn't have much longer. I think Ayanna and Cameron have an idea of how grave the situation is, but I haven't told Jada. Especially with the news of the baby and the fact that she wouldn't be able to fly out here for the funeral, I didn't want to upset her right now."

I shook my head. Jada was going to be devastated that she wouldn't be able to say goodbye to her grandmother. After a moment of hesitation, Julian spoke again.

"What's going on though?" he asked. "I appreciate you asking, but I know you didn't call me late at night about my mother's health."

I didn't know where to start, but I knew it was time to tell him everything.

"I don't know if you've had a chance to speak to Cameron yet," I started, "but Blue got hit at the old warehouse. He didn't make it."

"Shit!" Julian said. "What the hell happened?"

Julian listened intently as I recounted the events of the evening.

"What the hell?" Julian asked. "Did somebody get in contact with Rock?"

I sighed. "He's dead too," I answered. "Looks like someone broke into his spot and took him out. The news is saying that it appears to be a home invasion gone wrong."

"But you're convinced that something else is going on?" Julian asked.

"Yeah. We've been handling things in the A without really telling you everything that's going on while you're dealing with your mother's illness, but if things can potentially affect your family ... "

"My family?" Julian asked. "What's going on, Aaron?"

I spent the next several minutes telling Julian everything. I told him about the resistance I was getting from Cameron, every suspicious or unusual thing that had happened with the crew, and Cameron killing Carlos.

"Who the hell was Carlos working with?" Julian asked.

"Mikey and Michaela Pitt."

"*What?*" Julian asked in disbelief.

"Exactly," I said. "Look ... my Dad and Uncle Nate were able to find out that the Pitt twins are in Atlanta. It's not a paid job either, Julian. It's personal, and they're coming after your money and your people."

"That doesn't make any sense," Julian said.

"I didn't think so either, but my dad ain't never been wrong about something like this," I told him. "Julian, what connection do you have to the twins?"

"None," he answered quickly. "I've only ever used them once. I don't have any other affiliation with them."

I shook my head and sighed heavily. I had hoped that Julian would have a little more insight than he did.

"Alright, man ... my pops, Nate, Luke ... we're all on it. We've been making sure the team is more secure. What happened to Blue tonight shouldn't have happened," I told him. "That's why I'm headed back to Atlanta tomorrow. I'm also making sure your daughters are safe. They aren't too crazy about the added security measures, but I'm doing everything I can to make sure than we are safe instead of sorry. We don't know what the Pitt twins are trying to do. If their mission is personal, their attack could eventually be personal as well."

This time Julian released a deep sigh.

"Don't worry about your girls, man. I've got them. I promise. I would never let anything happen to Ayanna and definitely not Jada," I said. "Speaking of which, there's something else I wanted to talk to you about."

"What's that?" Julian asked.

"Jada ..." I started. "With the baby on the way and everything going on with the business, it's made me realize how much she means to me, and how much I truly care about your daughter. I want to do something to solidify the structure of our growing family."

"Is that so?" Julian asked. "What did you have in mind?"

I gripped my phone a little tighter and looked out in the night view of the ocean before me. Then, I proceeded to tell Julian about my plans.

SHANNON

*V*alentine's Day came and went, and it had been a major disappointment. I barely spoke to Cameron throughout the day but had hopes that he would at least make dinner plans for us. He didn't. In fact, he didn't even come home that night. He showed up the next morning while I was preparing for work with a tired looking bouquet of flowers and a more tired excuse. The truth was, I was the one who was truly tired.

I was tired of giving him my heart to step on it repeatedly. I loved him, but I was tired of all the drama. When he initially moved back home, there appeared to be a change in his behavior, and I hoped he would continue to our relationship a priority. He didn't. Instead, he had returned to his old ways of lying and putting me last. I was convinced that he was cheating. I didn't have any proof, but I was certainly looking for it. I wanted to be sure, because if he was cheating again, I was leaving him for good.

In the two weeks since Valentine's Day, things were definitely strained for us. He started coming home late if at all. I hadn't seen him in three days, and we hadn't spoken in two.

Aaron had arranged a surprise family gathering for Jada and reached out to invite me. Aaron hadn't spoken to Cameron in a few days either and wanted to know if we would be in attendance. The weight of the stress from the past few days had driven me to my breaking point. I was completely out of character doing things I never thought that I would.

I shifted in the passenger seat of my friend Alicia's Honda Accord. We were looking for Cameron. In an effort to not be spotted on our drive-by mission, Alicia offered to drive her car instead of us riding around town in mine. We went by Cameron's father's house, the new meeting house in East Atlanta, the body shop, and a few other places Cameron was known to hang out. I called him, but of course, he wasn't answering his phone. I felt like a complete idiot.

"Damn, Shan," Alicia said while we sat in the parking lot of a barbershop that he frequented. "What do you want to do now?"

I sighed and looked at my phone again. I had not received a phone call or text message from my boyfriend. I shrugged my shoulders and shook my head.

"I guess there isn't anything else to do. If I'm going to this family thing by myself tonight, I need to figure out what I'm going to wear and start getting ready," I said, looking at the time.

"Okay. We'll head back to your place," Alicia said as she started the car's engine. "Hell, maybe Cameron will surprise us and be waiting for you there."

"I doubt that," I mumbled as Alicia started to drive.

Alicia pulled out of the shopping center onto the main street when a thought hit me. There was one other place that popped into my mind. There was one last place I wanted to check before I headed home.

"Hey, I just thought of something," I told Alicia. "There's another place I want to go before we head back to my house."

"Cool. Tell me where to go."

I put the address in the GPS, and Alicia started towards our destination. Fifteen minutes later, we were turning into the neighborhood where Cameron's brother Deuce used to live. The anxiety that I felt caused my stomach to tighten into knots when we turned onto Deuce's street.

"Pull over right here," I instructed Alicia.

We stopped one house up on the opposite side of the street from Deuce's house. Not only was Cameron's Challenger parked in the driveway but there was also an unfamiliar 3-series BMW. I sat in silence for a moment. He was at the house avoiding me while he had company. I pulled out my cell phone to dial his number. Again, it went to voicemail.

"What do you want to do, Shan?" Alicia asked. "If you want to go over there, I'm down. We already know that he's here, and apparently he's not alone."

"I don't know. Give me a minute," I told her.

I needed a moment to think. What if I was overreacting? What if the BMW belonged to one of his business partners and not the alleged mistress that I had created in my mind? I already felt like a dumbass for riding around town looking for him. If he really gave a damn about me or our relationship, he would have called me back or come home. I was getting ready to tell Alicia to pull off and head to my house when the front door opened. I could not believe my eyes when a pretty brown-skinned chick with a natural hairstyle step out onto the porch with a wide smile on her face.

Oblivious to the fact that Alicia and I sat right across the street watching them, Cameron joined her on the porch with an equally wide smile of his own. I sat there motionless as I watched them engage in a brief conversation all while hugging and kissing on each other.

"Oh, hell no!" Alicia said as she pulled out her cell phone and started taking pictures.

"What are you doing?"

"Collecting your evidence," she said. "If you confront him later and he tries to deny it at least you will have the proof that he's a lying dirty dog."

I sat there silently in the passenger seat while I watched my man hug and kiss on another woman. Eventually, they said their goodbyes and the woman walked to her BMW and left, unaware of the fact that Alicia was snapping pictures of her. Cameron stood on the porch watching the BMW pull away. To add insult to injury, I looked on while he pulled out his cell phone and answered another call before going back into the house. He had ignored my calls all day. I couldn't even label my emotions in that moment.

"That's it," I heard myself say out loud. "I guess I found what I was looking for."

Alicia turned towards me with a sympathetic look on her face.

"I'm sorry, friend," she said, "but forget him. You've wasted enough time on him. Be done with him for real this time. You won't have any trouble finding someone better."

I wanted to tell Alicia that I didn't want to find someone else. I wanted Cameron, but I knew that over the last several months Cameron's actions had shown me way more than his words. He didn't want to be in a committed relationship with me. He did not love me the way that I loved him. So instead of telling Alicia that he was the only man I wanted, I simply nodded in response to her comment.

"Can you just take me home?" I asked quietly. "I need to get ready for tonight."

"Sure," Alicia said with sympathetic eyes as she started her car again. "Just make sure you let me know when you're ready to confront him. I've got these pictures for you, and I'll be there whenever you need me to help you move your stuff out of that asshole's house."

I nodded again and settled back into my seat while she started towards the house that Cameron and I shared.

JADA

"Jada! What are you doing up there?" Aaron called from downstairs. "Let's go!"

"I'm coming. Give me a minute."

I huffed as I fished through a box of cosmetics. It had been a few weeks since Aaron moved me into his house, and I still had things to unpack. The truth was the further my pregnancy progressed the less energy I had. The little bit of energy I had was reserved for work while I tried to get a ton of things accomplished in a little bit of time. I made a promise to Aaron that I would put myself on maternity leave by the time I hit the eight-month mark. I was looking for one of my favorite lip colors for our date night.

I quickly found the MAC lipstick and finished my makeup. Earlier in the day, Aaron had insisted that I get my hair and nails done. My hair was blow-dried straighter than I normally wore it and loose body curls were added. The prenatal vitamins had my hair, skin, and nails flourishing, and both my hair and nails were longer than they had been in years. I headed from the bathroom to the walk-in closet to step into a pair of Christian Louboutin heels that surprisingly still fit my swollen feet. I quickly checked my appearance in the full-length mirror – smoothing down the front of the curve-hugging short sleeve midi dress that I wore. I grabbed my YSL clutch, slipped into my coat, and made my way down to the foyer to meet an expectant Aaron. Dressed in a gray tailored suit with a white fitted button-down shirt, he had his hair pulled back into a smooth, low ponytail, and looked amazing.

"Well don't you look delicious," I said as I kissed him on the lips.

His lips pulled into a smile, displaying his dimples. "You're looking quite edible yourself," he said, taking my hand. "Come on. I don't want to be late."

Aaron led me out of the house and into his new Escalade that was waiting in the driveway. I had no idea where we were headed when Aaron started our drive. I stared out of the window while he toyed with the radio. My baby bump had drastically grown in the matter of a few weeks, and I felt a lot larger than six months. I was tired and uncomfortable, but I didn't want to say no to Aaron's invitation for a date night. We had been so busy that we absolutely needed a night to ourselves. Aside from the R&B music that quietly played in the truck, we rode in silence. Aaron's left hand gripped the steering wheel while he rested his right hand on my swollen belly. I smiled and covered his hand with mine.

When I first suspected I was pregnant, I was so nervous to tell Aaron. By that point, he had already shared with me how the stress of being a single father to Olivia made him question if he ever wanted any more kids. With the complications from my previous pregnancies, I didn't want to cause any additional stress to our already complicated relationship for a pregnancy that might not have made it to full term. I had no idea how he would react. However, the last few months he had exceeded whatever expectations I had. Even with all the drama from work and our families, Aaron had gone out of his way to put our unborn child and our relationship first.

I was happy. For the first time in a very long time, I could truly say that my heart was content.

Aaron quickly cut his eyes in my direction to see me staring, smiling silently at him.

"What's on your mind?" he asked before focusing his attention back towards the road ahead.

"Nothing ... Everything ... You ... Us," I answered. I caressed the side of his face with my free hand. He kissed it. "Just how much I love you, and how happy I am right now."

His signature half-smile pulled at his lips. "I love you too, mama. Whatever it takes … I gotta keep my babies happy."

I leaned my head against the headrest and looked at the road while he continued to drive. A few minutes later, he parked on the street outside of an unfamiliar warehouse building.

"Where are we?"

He shut the engine off and glanced at his watch before looking at me. "Come on. You'll see."

He made his way to my side of the truck, opening my door and helping me down from the vehicle. He held my hand while he led the way into the building. It was dark and empty but reminded me of a loft rental space used for a video shoot Vanessa starred in years earlier. Aaron led me to the elevator, and we stepped inside.

"You know … I've never met any woman like you before," he stated. He pressed the button to take us to the roof of the building. "Coming from the family I was born into I've always had an appreciation for a strong woman. I just didn't think I would be able to find one suitable enough to share my life with."

I turned my head to look at him. He was staring at the closed elevator doors in front of us.

"You broke the mold, mama. The fact that you're still standing after all that you've been through amazes me and proves just how tough you are," he said. "You're tough enough to handle your businesses, your family … hell, you're even tough enough to call me on my shit. You're compassionate and loyal. You've opened my heart in a way that I never thought it would be opened again."

His eyes locked with mine as the elevator doors opened. As we stepped out of the elevator on the roof, I smiled at the scene before me. The rooftop provided a perfect view of Atlanta's city skyline. Aaron had set the mood for a romantic date night by arranging to have the area decorated with candles and rose petals. I covered my mouth with my hands and gawked at my view. Aaron moved to stand in front of me.

"Aw, babe. You know these hormones have turned me into a big cry baby," I said as I felt myself getting teary-eyed. "It's beautiful."

"You're beautiful."

I kissed his lips. My stomach was huge, and I didn't feel beautiful. Aaron was convincing anyhow. He took my hand again before he continued to speak.

"Jada, without even trying you make me want to be the best version of myself. You complete a part of me that I didn't even know I was lacking," he said. "You're everything to me. Everything I thought I would never find. Everything I need by my side. Everything a wife should be."

A wife? I leaned my head to the side and blinked hard, unsure if I had heard him correctly. He let out a slight laugh at my reaction.

"I love you, mama. Without question and without hesitation," he said, "and I can't picture the rest of my life without you by my side. I just want to spend the rest of my days on this earth making you as happy as you've made me."

Simultaneously he went down on one knee and pulled a small velvet box out of his jacket .pocket. I'm pretty sure I stopped breathing.

"Jada Camille Reid, I love you more than any words could ever explain. Will you marry me?"

He opened the box revealing the most beautiful engagement ring I had laid eyes on. It was a cushion-cut center stone – at least ten carats in a pavé setting. My jaw dropped at its size. I was speechless and felt my eyes watering again.

Unable to get my words out as I choked back my tears I nodded until I could manage to say, "Yes, baby. Of course."

Aaron's face spread into the widest smile I had ever seen him display. He removed the ring from the box and slid it onto my finger. Standing up from his kneeling position, he pulled me into a tight hug. We shared a passionate kiss and then he whispered into my ear, "I can't wait to make you the new Mrs. Mercer."

I kissed him again. If this was what cloud nine felt like, I never wanted to come down. My pregnancy had already heightened my emotions, and in that moment, I was truly overcome by love, joy, and excitement for our future.

"She said yes y'all!" Aaron called over my shoulder.

I looked behind me to see a host of family and friends coming around from behind the wall where the elevator was located. I scanned the faces of the crowd that surrounded us with love. Our inner circle of friends, his parents, Olivia, Ayanna and Tony, Daniella, Vanessa and DJ, Luke, Shannon and others were all present. Regina and Cameron were noticeably missing, but I refused to let their absences bother me. There was nothing that could take away my happiness.

Looking radiant as ever, Sophia pulled me into a warm hug and kissed me on the cheek. "Mi amor, soy tan contendo."

"Thank you. I'm happy too," I told her as I wiped my eyes. "These are tears of joy right now."

One by one, members of the group hugged and kissed me. Ayanna approached me with her phone up to her ear. "Congrats, sis," she said. She handed me her cell. "It's Dad."

I took the phone from her hands, holding it up to my ear.

"Hey, Daddy," I spoke into the phone.

"Congratulations, baby girl," he said to me.

"Thank you. I wish you were here," I said honestly. I hadn't seen my dad in months, and I missed him terribly. "How's Nana doing?"

I didn't miss the hesitation on his end before he said, "She's hanging in there, but that's another conversation for another day. I'm so happy for you and Aaron, Jada. He loves you so much. This is what I always wanted for you."

"I know, daddy. I know."

It was crazy how life worked out. For years I was so consumed with thoughts of marriage that I was running in behind the wrong person. Nothing about my relationship with Israel was easy. Every day with Aaron wasn't easy but loving him was. Choosing to be his partner in life was easy. There was no doubt in my heart about our relationship. I finally stumbled upon the thing that my dad had always wanted for me – a love like he and my mother shared. It was a feeling that I never wanted to let go.

CAMERON

Since Blue's death, I replayed the shooting in my head over and over again. The more I analyzed those moments, the more I felt within my soul that those fatal bullets were meant for me. After finding out that Rock had been murdered as well, it was obvious that the men had shown up with the intent to kill. I just had a feeling they missed their target. As much as I doubted him in the beginning, I was starting to believe that Aaron and his father were correct. Something was wrong. If the Pitt twins were in fact after my family that would explain everything that was going on. That thought made me incredibly uneasy.

I started to question every business decision I made over the course of the previous year. I had to admit that I fucked up. I had come to accept the fact that the MP1 and MP2 that Carlos was in contact with had to be Mikey and Michaela Pitt. By bringing Carlos into our fold, I opened that door. I was the one to allow the Pitt twins to have an inside man and get closer to my business and my family. After the shooting that took Blue's life, I questioned whether there was another inside man. Had I brought someone else untrustworthy into our crew? There was no way that two complete strangers should have known who I was and where to pick up the product that night. The guilt that I felt was eating away at me. By surrounding myself with individuals that were working for the enemy, I made our organization vulnerable. I played a part in creating the dangerous and unpredictable situation that we were facing.

Thinking about the turmoil we dealt with also made me even angrier with Aaron. With the threats that the organization faced on a daily basis, I could not believe that he had the audacity to drag my sister even further into danger by asking her to be his wife. Being his wife would put an even bigger target on her back than she already had from carrying the Reid last name. I didn't care if she was having his child or not. I couldn't understand how he could claim to love her but put her life at risk at the same time. That didn't seem like love to me. There was no way I would have attended their engagement gathering.

Instead, I went home for the first time in a few days expecting to find Shannon there so I could get the impending argument over with. She had blown my phone up, and I knew that she would be pissed when she saw me. To my surprise, I arrived at an empty house. I figured that she went to the proposal without me. When she returned home a little before ten o'clock, I was in the living room stretched across the couch, watching television. She entered the house quietly, dropping her purse and keys on the table in the foyer. After kicking off her heels she walked into the living room, stopping at the end of the sofa that I was lying across.

"I'm surprised to see you here," she said to me.

"Why is that?" I asked in a nonchalant tone. "This is my house."

Shannon shook her head and let out a short laugh. "You sure don't act like it. You're barely here anymore. You've started staying out all night again … sometimes not coming home at all …" she let her voice trail off.

I looked at her without explaining my behavior in the previous few days.

"Cameron, where have you been?" she asked softly.

"I've been around," I answered, with a shrug of my shoulders. "I told you things have been crazy since Blue died."

"Uh-huh," Shannon responded in a tone that led me to think that she didn't believe me. "So, you haven't been fucking around on me with some big butt chick with a natural."

I sat up straight on the couch.

"What are you talking about?"

"I'm talking about you fucking another bitch in your dead brother's house," she said. "That's what the fuck I'm talking about."

I exhaled deeply before standing up from the couch and walking towards her.

"Shannon, I know you're upset that I haven't been home, but don't come in here talking crazy," I told her. "You're always so goddamn quick to jump to conclusions."

"It's not crazy talk when I have proof," she stated firmly.

Proof? I didn't have a clue in hell what she was talking about. I had been messing around with Brianna for nearly a year, and I was pretty careful. I didn't know what proof she could have been talking about, so I shook my head and waved her off.

"I don't know what the hell you're talking about, but I didn't come home tonight to do this arguing shit with you," I said.

Instead of responding right away, Shannon lifted her phone and started to scroll through it. I had no idea what she was looking for, but I was starting to get nervous. It was obvious she knew about Brianna and that I had been at Deuce's house. I had no idea what she could have seen or heard.

"That's fine. You can go back over to Deuce's house to meet

up with your side bitch," she said as she shoved her cell phone into my face. "Isn't that where you were earlier today?"

I looked at the picture on her screen of me kissing Brianna on the porch of Deuce's house earlier that day.

Fuck. I had no idea how I was going to get out of this one.

"What the fuck is this?" I asked her.

"You tell me Cameron!" she shouted. "How long have you been fucking this bitch?"

"You fucking stalking me now?" I asked instead of answering her question. "Where the hell did you get this picture?"

"That's not the point. That's not the fucking point!" she yelled. "That's you! That is obviously you touching some bitch that ain't me!"

I continued to hold the phone, staring at the picture and ignoring Shannon's words.

"How could you do this to me? *Me!* Cameron, I've been there for you through everything that has happened over the last few years!" she screamed as she pushed me in my chest.

I barely moved. Instead, my jaw clenched while I started to get a headache. She didn't answer my question. If Shannon was riding around town following me, there was no telling what she knew or what she could have seen. The thought of not knowing exactly what she knew gave me an uneasy feeling. For the first time in our relationship, I was starting to feel like she couldn't be trusted either.

"You're just going to stand there and not say anything?" Shannon asked. "You have nothing to say for yourself?"

"What do you want from me, Shannon?" I yelled back at her. "You've accused me of cheating on you from the beginning, and now you finally got what you wanted. Are you happy now?"

"Am I happy now? What kind of question is that?" Shannon asked.

"I don't know, Shan. You thought this has been going on for a while and now you finally have your proof," I told her. "Do you want the details too? Do you want to know all about her, and how I've been fucking her for months?"

Shannon slapped me across the face.

"Fuck you!" she shouted.

"Nah fuck you!" I shouted back at her. I threw her cell phone across the room where it hit the wall and broke into a few pieces. "You ain't been nothin' but a pain in my ass for months. I ain't doing this shit with you no more!"

I stepped back into my shoes, grabbed my keys, and slipped into my coat.

"So, because I'm a pain in the ass you cheated on me and ruined our relationship for what? For an ego boost?" Shannon asked.

I started towards the front door. The last thing I wanted was to keep going back and forth with her. She continued to speak to my back.

"Do whatever you need to do to pump yourself up!" she yelled. "You can fuck all the bitches you want, but you still ain't gonna be a boss. You'll never be your father, Cameron. Even after Deuce got killed, your dad still didn't put you in a position of power. You have to play a secondary role to your sister's baby daddy. So, if this bitch makes you feel better about yourself, then by all means go right ahead. Blow her fucking back out for all I care. I'm sick of this shit! I'm sick of you!"

With my hand on the doorknob, I froze. Shannon knew how to get under my skin and had always been an expert at pressing my buttons. She had gone too far this time. I had planned to go back to Deuce's house or Brianna's place to give Shannon to spend the rest of the night to cool off. Her words had changed my plans. I wasn't going anywhere. I turned back around to face her.

"You know what? I was just about to leave," I told her, "but then I just remembered that this is my shit. I may not be a boss, but my money paid for this damn house. I'm not going anywhere, but you can leave! If you're so goddamn sick of me, get your shit and get the fuck out!"

"What?" Shannon asked with wide eyes.

"You heard what I said," I answered in a calm tone. I opened the door and flung it open. "Get your purse and your keys and get the fuck out of my house. Maybe you can go find you a boss ass nigga to put a roof over your head."

Shannon stood there looking at me in disbelief. I grabbed her by the arm and drug her towards the front door. I shoved her onto the porch and then grabbed her purse, keys, and shoes. Ignoring the tears in her eyes, I threw her things at her and slammed the door in her face.

MICHAELA

Things were moving according to my new plan – slowly but surely. Being the more restless one between the two of us, Mikey was growing impatient. He didn't like Atlanta and wanted to get back to DC as soon as possible. I, on the other hand, had way more patience. I didn't care how much time it took as long as we achieved success. I was prepared to stay in Atlanta as long as I needed until Julian Reid and everything he had built was destroyed.

I sat behind the driver's seat of a rented Toyota Camry with Mikey in the passenger seat. We were parked across the street from Jada's restaurant, Carmen's, where we followed Cameron. We had trailed him for the better part of the day unnoticed. I already knew from our inside man, Dre, that the Reid organization increased security on all levels. However, Cameron would have made it obvious. He was no longer riding around in his beloved Dodge Challenger. Instead, he was being chauffeured in a large black SUV with at least two other men riding along with him.

One of the guys waited outside the front of the restaurant

while Cameron went inside for a brief moment. He came back out, waiting by his vehicle for a few moments. The restaurant was on a busy street. If Cameron was half as smart as I believed him to be, he would not have been hanging out so casually on a busy street without knowing who was watching him or passing by. He obviously had no idea that Mikey and I had eyes on him. He was going to make our job easy – a little too easy.

Almost as if he were reading my mind, Mikey smirked and said, "Look at this fool. If we wanted, we could take him out right now before his goons could even get out of the truck."

"I know," I agreed.

Before I could say anything else, I watched the door to the restaurant opened and saw Jada Reid joined her brother in front of the restaurant. However, she was not alone. She had a look of irritation on her face as she approached her brother with a tall, muscular man following her. I figured that he was her security. Her bodyguard was more interested in their surroundings than the intense conversation I was witnessing between Julian's two youngest children. While I continued to watch the siblings go back and forth, I noticed two things – one was the surprising presence of a baby bump and the other being a sizeable diamond ring on her left hand.

"Damn. I had no idea she was pregnant," Mikey said.

"Me either," I commented. "I also had no idea that she was engaged. I can see that rock from all the way over here."

Mikey and I both looked on while Jada threw her hand up to wave Cameron off dismissively.

"Shit. Dre definitely didn't tell us that," Mikey said. "I guess Aaron Mercer decided to go ahead and wife her up. She's fine as hell though. If I were him, I would lock that down too."

I cut my eyes at my brother. "Nigga, I don't care how attractive she is. That ain't got shit to do with why we are here," I snapped at him.

170

Mikey shrugged his shoulders. "I was just making an observation. Damn."

"What you need to be concerned about is the fact that she just became the most valuable Reid," I told him. "I thought taking out Cameron would be the best decision, because that would kill Julian's legacy."

"But now …?"

"Cameron hasn't been very useful to anyone lately," I told my brother. "Dre said that Aaron is actually the one running the business. Whatever power we thought Cameron had apparently went out the window months ago."

"So, you want to change the plan again?" Mikey sighed.

"Not the plan. Just the intended target," I said as I turned back towards the siblings that were still going back and forth on the sidewalk of a busy Buckhead street. Julian would be so disappointed if he were there to witness it. With my eyes on the pair, I continued to speak to my brother. "I think taking out his baby girl would hurt Julian much more than killing his idiot son."

Mikey shook his head. "Damn, Michaela. She's pregnant, and the Mercers never did anything to us," he said.

"This isn't about the Mercers. This is about the Reids. Technically she is still a Reid," I answered him, "and I don't give a fuck about her baby."

"That's cold-blooded," Mikey said.

"Are we on the same team or not?" I asked him with narrowed eyes.

"Of course we are," he said. "I just think you're going a little overboard. She can't even talk to her brother without security over her shoulder. Why in the world do you think Aaron would ever allow us to get close to her? He's sharper than that – much smarter than Cameron has been acting. We can just stick with the original idea of taking out Cameron and be back home in no time. He's making this easier than either of us thought it would be."

"I don't want to take the easy approach. Mike, you know I've always liked a challenge. You're right though. Killing Jada Reid will not be easy," I said as I started the engine and pulled away from the restaurant, "but my brother it will be so worth it. Just trust me."

JADA

I laid across our bed with my back towards the door while I heard Aaron's footsteps approaching. I assumed he stopped in the doorway but didn't say anything. For the last few days he had gone out of his way to try to cheer me up since my grandmother had succumbed to her cancer. It was one thing to lose my grandmother, but my grief was compounded by the fact that I was unable to attend her funeral. While Ayanna, Tony, my aunts, and even Cameron were in route to California, I was stuck in Atlanta because my doctor had not cleared me to travel. Nana Reid and I had always shared a special bond and not being able to be there with the rest of my family was incredibly upsetting.

"Hey," Aaron eventually said.

I sighed. "Hey," I said, rolling onto my other side to face him.

"You got any plans today?" he asked. "I know you've been in the house the last couple of days. Are going into work?"

I shook my head. "No. We have more than enough staff at the salon until Yanni gets back. With the management staff I have in place right now, the restaurant and boutique are pretty

173

much operating on autopilot," I answered. "I don't really feel like doing anything today."

"Vanessa hit me up a little bit ago. She said she's been trying to get ahold of you," Aaron said.

I shrugged my shoulders. "I don't even know where my phone is right now."

Outside of my fiancé, I didn't feel like being bothered.

"Why don't you use mine and call her back?" he suggested as he walked closer to the bed. He sat down next to me and handed me his cell. "Maybe lunch and shopping with your girl will help take your mind off of things."

I wanted to protest his suggestion, but I didn't. I knew that he was only trying to make me feel better. I sat up in the bed and took the phone from his hands. I let out another sigh before dialing Vanessa's number.

"Hello," she answered.

"Hey, Ness. It's me."

"Jada, hey! I think you should get dressed so we can get out of the house for a little bit," she suggested.

"Sure, that sounds fine," I responded. There was no enthusiasm in my voice, but Vanessa didn't care.

"Great, because I'm already on the way over," she said. "Let Aaron know that I'll be there in about ten minutes so he can let me in through the gate. See you soon!"

I ended the call and relayed the message to Aaron. He went into the bathroom and started the shower. I scooted to the edge of the bed and sat there for a minute before joining him in the bathroom. He already had a towel and washcloth waiting for me.

"We just want to put a smile back on your face, mama," he said. "Indulge her. If you're not feeling it after a little bit, just shoot me a text, and the driver will bring you right back home. Go on and hop in the shower while I try to find your phone."

He kissed my cheek and left me alone in our bathroom.

After a hot shower, I found something to wear. I was always a believer that if you looked good, you would eventually feel good as well. I desperately wanted to feel good. Between the grief over the loss of Nana and my fatigue from the pregnancy, I felt like crap. There was no way I was going to go in public reflecting that.

After dressing in a mustard yellow Ingrid & Isabel maternity maxi dress, I applied my makeup and brushed my hair back into a ponytail. I slipped my feet into my Tory Burch flats and grabbed my jacket before heading down the stairs where Aaron and Vanessa were chatting in the kitchen.

"You look cute," Vanessa greeted me with a wide smile.

"Yeah, babe. You look good," Aaron said, winking at me.

"Thanks."

Both Vanessa and Aaron stood up from their stools at the kitchen island. Vanessa put her jacket on while Aaron walked over to me.

"Here," he said, handing me the phone. "Scott is going to drive you to the mall. It's still kind of early so hopefully, it won't be too crowded. I'm still sending Harold and Vic with y'all, and no it's not up for discussion. They are already waiting in the truck."

Aaron shut down my objection before I could even voice it. I had hoped that whatever was going on with work that caused all the extra security would have died down by now, but it was apparent that it had not.

"Try to enjoy yourself," he said. "I have to step out and handle some things, but just let Scott know when you're ready to come home. Alright?"

I nodded in agreement.

"Love you," he said before kissing me on the lips.

"Love you too."

I put on my jacket and walked with Vanessa to the driveway where our driver Scott was waiting beside the Escalade. He helped us into the vehicle and made sure that we were settled before starting towards the mall.

"Oh! You never finished telling me what happened when Cameron popped up at the restaurant last week," Vanessa said.

I rolled my eyes. "Girl, the boy has lost his damn mind," I told her. "You know that we've barely spoken since he found out I was pregnant, but he showed up at the restaurant saying that we needed to talk."

"What for and why now?"

"Because he and Shannon broke up a couple of weeks ago – the night Aaron and I got engaged. He said he doesn't want me talking to her anymore," I said.

"Seriously?" Vanessa asked with a frown. "First, he can't tell you who you can and cannot be friends with. Second, haven't they been off and on a lot recently? They will probably be back together next week?"

"I don't know about that," I said. "I talked to Shannon the other day, and she's pretty much done with him. He cheated on her ... again ... and then threw her out of their house. She's been staying with a friend."

"That's too much drama for me," Vanessa said. "Don't let Cameron stress you out, girl. All you need to be concerned about is making sure that my little niece or nephew continues to bake and that you start wedding planning. Speaking of the wedding, where is that rock, girl?"

I looked down at my swollen hands.

"At the house. My hands have been swelling."

"I thought you were going to tell me that you couldn't wear it all the time because that rock was too damn heavy," Vanessa teased.

I flashed a smile at her. "He did good, didn't he?"

"Hell yeah, he did!" Vanessa laughed.

We continued to laugh and talk the rest of the way to the mall. Aaron and Vanessa were right. Getting out of the house had done wonders for my mood. Of course, I was still sad I was missing my Nana's funeral, but some girl talk and a little retail therapy helped. When we got to the mall, I followed Vanessa while she bounced from store to store. Wherever we went our security – Harold and Vic – were right there. I looked down at the watch on my wrist and saw that it almost two o'clock in the afternoon. Time had passed by quickly. I ran my fingers through my ponytail and let out a deep sigh. I was not feeling great when I woke up that morning but agreed to go shopping anyway. Almost three hours later, I was starving and ready to cut our shopping trip short.

"Ness ... how much longer?" I whined. "I'm ready to eat."

Vanessa laughed as she thumbed through the racks of designer jeans. "Honey, you're always ready to eat these days. That is nothing new," she said. "Let me just see if they have my size and then we can ..."

Vanessa stopped mid-sentence as she stared behind me towards the entrance of Nordstrom. I frowned and looked over my shoulder to see what captured Vanessa's attention. It was Israel Mann, and he was making his way into the department store. He spoke on his cell phone until he glanced in our direction. The moment that our eyes met; he froze in his tracks. After a moment of hesitation, he ended his phone call and slowly made his way over to Vanessa and me. He stopped just a few feet away, and his eyes dropped as I nervously rubbed my baby bump.

This was it. This was the moment that I was dreading although I couldn't explain why. I never responded to Israel's text from the night I met Aaron. I hadn't seen Israel since the day he left for Texas. I knew that he would be back in town at some point. Atlanta was big and small at the same time. Hell, his grandmother and I were still members at the same church – although I hadn't been in months. I knew that there was a possibility I would run into Israel at some point. I just never imagined that it would be in the middle of a department store when I was seven months pregnant with another man's child.

"Damn," Israel mumbled with his eyes still focused on my stomach.

Vanessa cleared her throat to redirect his attention. "Israel, wow. Long time no see. I didn't even know that you were in town," she said as she stepped around me and hugged her old friend.

"Yeah," he said. "I just got here actually. I'm just stopping by the mall to grab something to wear for this party I'm headed to a little later."

"Cool. Where's the party? I'm looking to get into something later," Vanessa said.

"Well it's actually a little family thing with …" his voice trailed off as he looked back at my stomach. "Do you mind if I speak with Jada for a minute?"

The two goons that Aaron sent for our protection took a step forward. Israel's eyes widened and Vanessa turned around to wave Harold and Vic off.

"Chill," Vanessa said with annoyance. "He's harmless. He's practically family. You can call your boss and ask him if need be. He knows who Israel is."

Harold and Vic exchanged uneasy glances but took a slight step backwards.

"I promise its fine," I told them. "I'll be right back."

Vanessa turned back towards the rack of jeans. When I turned back towards Israel, I motioned towards the store's café.

"Let's head over there and grab a seat. I'm starving and Ness is holding me hostage. I at least need something to drink," I told Israel.

He nodded and followed me to the store's restaurant. After grabbing a drink, we found a table towards the back of the dining room. Israel pulled my chair out for me before taking his own seat across the table.

"So ..." he said.

"Yeah ..." I said, rubbing my stomach again.

"I guess congratulations are in order," Israel said as he motioned towards my stomach. "Who's the lucky guy? If you don't mind me asking."

I hesitated and looked away from Israel before answering. "Aaron Mercer."

"Must be two Aaron Mercers," Israel quickly responded.

I was silent. Israel shook his head in disbelief.

"Aaron Mercer as in *the* Aaron Mercer? Son of Manny Mercer?" he asked.

"That would be the one," I said as I took a sip of my drink.

"Damn," Israel said, leaning back from the table. "You sure know how to pick 'em, huh?"

"Wow," I said. "Maybe this was a mistake."

Israel reached across the table to grab my hand, but I pulled away from him. "Jada, I'm sorry. I had no right to go there."

"No Israel. You didn't have a right to go there at all, but somehow we always end up here, don't we?" I said, still shaking my head. "The truth is that you left me. Again. You packed your things, sold your house, got your GM to stop your trade to Atlanta, and left me for good. Even after finding out that I was pregnant and later that I had a miscarriage, you still didn't reach out to me. Don't judge what has happened in your absence."

Israel shook his head. "You're right. I'm sorry," he said. "It got to the point where it was just too much. Caleb, Kelvin, Deuce, everything I ever did to you ... I didn't think we were ever going to get over it."

"Who knows?" I shrugged my shoulders. "Maybe you're right."

We sat quietly for a few moments before Israel spoke again.

"Look, Jada ... there's something I need to tell you," he stated.

Israel paused. I studied his face and could tell that whatever he had to say was not going to be easy for him. I leaned back in my seat. I knew that if it was hard for him to say, it would be even harder for me to hear.

"What is it?" I asked after a few more moments.

Israel, who had been looking down at his hands, looked up and directly into my eyes. "The reason I'm back in town this weekend. It's for my engagement party."

"Engagement?"

"Yeah …" Israel looked back down at his hands. "Angelina's family is throwing us an engagement party tonight. I won't even be in town for a full twenty-four hours, Jay. I tried to reach out to you a while ago … I admit that I could have handled our situation better. Sometimes when I think about the way things ended up between us, I honestly don't know how we got here. I never would have pictured things turning out this way."

I drew in a sharp breath. After I heard Israel say Angelina's name, I honestly didn't hear much else. Yes, I was getting ready to have a child by someone else. Had my hands not been swollen that morning I would have worn my engagement ring and Israel would have known that I would also be walking down the aisle soon. None of that made it any less painful to hear that the man that I had loved for the better part of a decade – the man that I had grown up with – was getting ready to marry another woman.

"Angelina?" I asked, blinking back tears. Those damn pregnancy hormones were starting to get to me again.

Israel sighed and reached across the table for my hand. I took a deep breath to calm myself. The last thing I needed to do was stress myself out and have to explain to Aaron what had gotten me so upset.

"I don't know what to say to that," I said with teary eyes. "Angelina? Maybe I shouldn't feel any type of way about you getting married, because it's clear that I have moved on as well, but dammit, man."

"Jada, I can't tell you how you should feel. Regardless of

where we are in our lives today, you and I have a lot of history. I have to admit that seeing you pregnant by another man is kind of messing with me. I loved you. You have to know that," he said, "but Jada ... she's the one."

In a strange way, I appreciated his honesty. Given the ups and downs of the most recent years of our lives, his truth was kind of sobering. Even still, the impact of his words hit me like a ton of bricks and there was an uncomfortable tightness in my chest. I wasn't sure if this was a normal reaction for a woman that was engaged to marry another man. Israel's use of the word "loved" made it perfectly clear to me that our love story had finally reached its conclusion. In the back of my mind, I already knew it, but now I had no other choice but to accept it as reality.

I pushed away from the table and rose to my feet. Israel stood up as well.

"Well, I don't want to hold you," I said. "Take care."

I turned on my heels and left. With each step away from Israel, I knew that this was it. I finally had the closure I never received. There were no more business connections between Israel and my father. There would be no more holiday gatherings between mutual friends. The sale had been finalized on Israel's suburban Atlanta home, and his new life was taking him 785 miles away for good. Besides televised football games and gossip blogs, I knew that it could possibly be the last time I saw Israel Mann. I resisted the urge to look over my shoulder at him one last time before I made my way back to Vanessa.

"Are you okay?" she asked.

I nodded. "Yeah. I am," I answered her, "but I want to go home. Can we just grab something to eat and head back to the house?"

"Of course," Vanessa said. "I promised Aaron I would get you back home if you weren't feeling it."

As we headed back to the car, I texted Aaron to let him know that Scott was taking us home. He responded by telling me that he was working with plans to be home before dinner, but if I need him to come home sooner to let him know. I breathed a sigh of relief knowing that I had a few hours to get over my final encounter with Israel before my fiancé arrived home.

AARON

I arrived home shortly before eight o'clock. Knowing that Jada wasn't feeling very social the last few days, I had given our housekeeper, Julissa, the day off – opting to pick up dinner on my way in. My day was long but smooth. In all honesty, things were somewhat quiet since Blue's death. It was so quiet in fact that I started to wonder if the Pitt twins gave up and went back to DC. After making sure that the money from the week was okay, I gave Luke the weekend off. He had not been back home to Miami in a while, and I knew that he wanted to see his family and Nakia.

After parking in the garage, I entered the house with takeout bags from Jada's favorite Chinese restaurant. Harold and Vic were still there since they were being paid to say with Jada whenever I was not around. They were hanging around the kitchen – Vic was monitoring the security cameras from his tablet while Harold read a newspaper. I greeted them both as I sat my food on the counter.

"What's up?"

"Nothing much, man," Harold said, looking up from his paper. "It was a pretty quiet day."

"Yeah. We probably got back from the mall around three-thirty," Vic chimed in. "Her friend Vanessa just left about an hour ago. Jada's up in your room."

"Cool. I got some extra food if either of you want to eat before you head out," I said.

Vic stood up from the eat-in kitchen table and shook his head. "Nah, man. I'm good, but I appreciate it."

"Same here," Harold said as he closed his paper and stood up from the kitchen island stool. "Let us know what time you need us in the morning."

"Will do," I said as I slapped hands with both men and sent them on their way.

I quickly made our plates before climbing the stairs with a serving tray. When I made it to our bedroom, I paused in the doorway observing Jada while she lay in bed looking at her iPad. A few seconds later, she looked up and smiled when she noticed me. I made my way over to her, sitting the tray on my bedside table before sitting down beside her and kissing her forehead. Even at seven months pregnant, tired with no makeup, she was still one of the most beautiful women I had laid eyes on. Paired with the fact that she was equally as beautiful on the inside, I knew that I was a lucky man.

"Hey, baby," she greeted me with a smile.

"Hey ... what are you looking at?" I asked, peeking at her iPad.

"Some pregnancy app thing," she answered. "Did you know that the baby is already the size of a head of celery?"

"Nah," I laughed. "I had no idea."

"What do you have over there?" she asked, pointing to the tray of food.

"Dinner from one of your favorite places," I replied as I reached for the tray and set it in her lap.

"Oh, baby! Thank you!" she said before kissing me on the lips. "I did not feel like going down those steps for food."

"Now you don't have to," I said. I watched her grab an egg roll and take a bite. "I forgot our drinks. I'll be right back."

I was halfway down the stairs when my phone started ringing. I was going to ignore it until I saw that it was my father trying to reach me.

"Pops, what's up?" I answered the call while I walked up to the refrigerator.

My dad released a deep breath on the other end of the line. I paused with the refrigerator door wide open.

"Black, your Uncle Nate and I got some more information about the Pitt twins," he said.

There was a level of concern in his voice that I had not heard in years. My father was one of the most levelheaded, even-keeled men that I knew. His news had to be major if I was able to detect the concern in his voice.

"What's going on?" I asked.

"The Pitt twins are coming after Jada."

"Huh?" I asked in disbelief. "You sure about that? How did you even find that out?"

He sighed again before he continued to speak. "They have another inside man. Carlos wasn't the only one. There's apparently some kid named Dre that's been working with them for months," he said. "Dre isn't as sharp or discreet as Carlos was. I'm actually surprised that the Pitts chose him to be on their team, but anyway ... he's been running his mouth a little too much. Your Uncle found one of his friends and got him to talk. Apparently, the plan was to kill Cameron since they couldn't get to Julian. I don't know why, but Dre said the twins changed the plan. They're coming after Jada now. It turns out that their mission was personal from the start as we thought. Everything they did to fuck with the business was to distract you, Cameron, and everyone else. They were paying themselves by taking money out of your pockets while planning to kill one of Julian's kids."

"But Jada though? That doesn't make any sense. What the fuck does she have to do with any of this?"

My stomach felt uneasy.

"It's their way of getting at Julian," he answered. "It's their way to destroy him ... by any means necessary."

"She's pregnant though. What the fuck?" I questioned in frustration.

"You know Michaela is ice cold. I guarantee you she's not thinking about your child," my father said.

"I swear to God if she lays a finger on Jada, I will kill her and her goddamn brother myself," I said with a clenched jaw.

"Look, I'm not telling you this so you can fly off at the handle and do something irrational," I heard my dad say. "I'm telling you so that you can make sure Jada is protected around the clock. I know you've stepped up the security, but we need to take it to another level until we can figure out how to handle this. The Hit twins don't miss, Black. If we are going to get them before they get to her, we need to have a plan – a well thought out plan free of emotion."

"Yeah alright," I responded.

"Aaron, I am serious. Don't do anything stupid. There's no way you need to go looking for the twins by yourself. Until we have more information stay focused and protect your woman," my father said.

"I hear you," I said firmly.

"Alright. Let me get up with Nate. I'll talk to you soon."

I ended the call and gripped my phone tightly while I stood in front of the refrigerator. I ran a hand over my face to muffle the string of curse words that came out of my mouth. I couldn't let Jada see my frustration. There weren't even enough words to express the frustration I felt anyway. There was no way I was going to lose my woman and my unborn child at the hands of Michaela Pitt. I would die before I allowed her to harm them.

My ringing cell phone disturbed my thoughts. It was Jada.

"Did you get lost on the way to the kitchen?" she joked after I answered her call.

I forced a laugh. "My bad, mama. I took a phone call that ran longer than I thought it would. I'm headed back up right now."

I grabbed two bottles of water and jogged back up the stairs.

"I hope you didn't want any Crab Rangoon," she said with a mouth full of food. "Because I just ate the ones on both plates."

I shrugged my shoulders and sat down on the bed. "What's mine is yours," I told her.

Jada snapped her fingers and pointed in my direction. "Look at you getting prepared for married life already," she laughed.

After speaking to my father, she had no idea how ready for marriage I was. Just in case I lost my life in the process of trying to save hers, I wanted to make sure that everything I had belonged to Jada and our kids. There was only one way to legally ensure that happened.

"Speaking of marriage," I started, "I want to get your thoughts on something."

"Yeah. What's that?" Jada asked as she forked more food into her mouth.

"I want to get married before the baby comes."

Jada stopped chewing and looked at me with a frown. "We've only been engaged for a month. Are you serious?" she asked. "I doubt I can even plan a wedding in eight weeks, babe."

"We can go to the courthouse."

Jada's frown deepened. "The courthouse? Do you even know me at all?"

I laughed. I knew that was not how she pictured her big day. I knew that she wanted a big wedding that was over the top and beautiful – just like her.

"I don't care where we get married, mama. I just want to make it official," I told her. "We can do the big wedding next year."

Jada sat back against the pillows and stared at me for a moment.

"You're serious?" she asked.

"As a heart attack."

She was quiet for a few more moments before she finally said, "Okay. Let's do it."

"Yeah?" I asked to make sure she was certain.

"Yes."

I leaned across the bed and kissed her on the lips. When I pulled away, Jada spoke again.

"We can get married at the courthouse, but baby ... you better be ready to swipe that AMEX next year. The ceremony is going to be major."

"I have no doubt," I laughed as I reached for my plate of food.

SHANNON

"Here you go, girl," Alicia said.

She handed me a glass of wine and sat down next to me on the sofa. I had been at her place since the night Cameron threw me out of the house that he made clear belonged to him and him alone. After he broke my phone, I replaced it and changed my number. However, Cameron still found a way to get in contact with me. The few conversations we had turned into arguments. I was tired, and I was over it. I was sad that I wasted the last two and half years on him, but I knew I needed to let it go and move on.

"I just can't believe him. Everything you two have been through, and he pulls some shit like this," our friend Keri said as she shook her head. "That nigga has a lot of nerve."

Keri joined us for a girl's night in. We ordered pizza and were supposed to be watching movies. Instead, we overindulged in wine and were talking about my drama.

"I just knew that something was wrong," I told her. "He

started with that disrespectful shit again. Not answering his phone. Not coming home at night. I had a feeling that maybe he was cheating, but honestly, I don't think I would have really believed it if I hadn't seen it with my own two eyes."

"Speaking of seeing it with your own eyes, you said you had pictures of the bitch," Keri said. "Let me see this ho. I bet she's not even pretty."

"Cameron broke her phone, but I still have the pictures on mine," Alicia said as she opened her photo gallery and passed the phone to Keri.

Keri sat on the loveseat scrolling through the photos with a frown on her face. I didn't know if she was just trying to make me feel better. I had seen Cameron's side bitch in person. She wasn't ugly – far from it actually. I didn't need my friends to lie about her appearance thinking that it was going to make me feel better. Cameron had lied enough for everybody.

"She looks real familiar," Keri said when she looked up from Alicia's phone. "Like I feel like I know her. Do you know her name?"

I shook my head. "No," I answered. "Cameron won't even talk about her. He said his personal business has nothing to do with me anymore."

Alicia rolled her eyes and took a sip of her wine. Keri looked back down at the pictures as she started to scroll through them again. I guzzled my wine, emptying the glass in one long sip.

"When are you going to get the rest of your things from over there?" Alicia asked.

I shrugged my shoulders. "I don't know. Every time I ask Cam, he comes up with another excuse for why I can't come over," I answered. "I almost want to just say fuck it. I have enough money to replace the little bit of shit that's still there."

"You shouldn't have to," Alicia said. "He's the one that cheated, but he's been acting like you're the one that did him wrong. You still have your key, don't you?"

"Yes, I do, but I'm not trying to go over there at the wrong time and start another fight with him," I said. "Do you know how embarrassing it was for him to throw me out of the house like that?"

Alicia shook her head.

"He grabbed me by my arm and literally threw me out of the house ... barefoot ... in the cold. He threw my purse and my keys at me and slammed the door in my face," I told her. "I'm not trying to go through that again. I was in shock the first time but thinking about it now just pisses me off. I'm so mad at him that I don't even know what would happen if I saw him right now."

Out the corner of my eye, I saw Keri's mouth fall open as she sat up and leaned forward on the couch.

"What's wrong with you?" Alicia asked.

Keri turned to look at me, shaking her head with a look of disbelief on her face.

"I know who she is," she said.

"You know who she is?" I asked Keri.

"I mean ... I don't know her that well, but yeah ... I know why she looked so familiar," Keri answered. "I know who she is."

"Okay then spill it," Alicia said. "Who the hell is she?"

Keri looked at Alicia, but then cut her eyes back towards me.

"Shannon ... before I tell you who she is I need to know ... how mad are you at Cameron?" she asked.

I frowned. "I'm pissed."

"Are you sure that you're done with him?" she asked.

"Yes," I answered quickly. "I still care about him, but there's no coming back from this. There's no forgiving what he did to me."

Keri let out a deep breath. "Okay ... she was at my cousin's ugly sweater Christmas party. She works with my cousin, Shan."

"Which cousin?" I asked her.

"Trent. This chick works with Trent. That's how I know her,

Shannon," Keri said. "I've probably seen her around before, but I am certain this is the girl from that party. I can ask Trent to be sure if you want me to ..."

"Holy shit!" Alicia yelled.

I felt the air being sucked from my lungs as Keri continued to explain just how she had come into contact with Cameron's side chick. Alicia and I both knew where Trent worked. I honestly could not believe the words that were coming out of Keri's mouth.

CAMERON

*C*overing my mouth with one of my hands, I yawned before looking at the time on my clock. It was almost ten o'clock in the morning, and I was going to need to start my day soon. I looked down at Brianna who was still peacefully sleeping next to me in my bed. In the month or so since Shannon and I split, Brianna had pretty much taken her place. Being that I didn't have to sneak around or hide her anymore, she was spending more time at my place than hers. I was thankful for Brianna's presence, because it distracted me from how much I missed Shannon. I thought that as the weeks passed I would easily be able to get over Shannon, but that hadn't happened. I still cared about her, but I didn't trust her. Love cannot exist where there is no trust.

I sat up in the bed, swinging my legs over the side and sliding to the edge. I had just gotten back in town from Nana's funeral the evening before, and even though I was tired I knew that there was business to handle. I was supposed to meet with PO, Luke, and Aaron to determine who would permanently be in charge of the muscle now that Blue was gone. I knew that decision would ultimately be made by Aaron, but I was glad to at least be included. With the pushback that I gave Aaron over the last several months, it was a wonder that he dealt with me at all.

My father was still in California with intentions to stay a little longer to wrap up some of Nana's personal affairs. Before I returned to Atlanta, he pulled me to the side and gave me an earful about my behavior since he left. At the age of twenty-six, it did not feel good to still receive lectures from my father, but I can't say that he was wrong. I was at the place where I could accept responsibility for my actions. The more I spoke to my dad the more I started to realize that he actually might be considering stepping away from the drug business. Without him or Deuce around to be involved in that side of the business, I knew I ultimately had no choice but to try to make things amicable with Aaron. Especially since Aaron and Jada had opted for a quickie courthouse wedding in another two weeks. It wasn't ideal nor the way I ever would have imagined things working out, but it seemed as if I had no choice but to accept it as reality.

"Hey, you," I heard Brianna's voice behind me.

I turned to look at her over my shoulder while she slowly sat up in the bed. "Good morning," I greeted her.

"What do you have planned for your day?" she asked.

"Got a meeting in a little bit," I answered. "I was getting ready to hop in the shower."

"Want some company?" she asked with a mischievous grin.

I smiled back at her. "You know I ain't never going to turn that down," I told her. "Come on."

Brianna climbed out of the bed and joined me for a hot shower. After we finished, I handed her a towel and we stood in the bathroom drying our bodies. Brianna wrapped her towel around her before wrapping her arms around me.

"You sure you have to go to this meeting?" she asked.

"Yeah. There's some shit going on. I have to meet up with the guy."

"Who all are you meeting with?" Brianna asked.

"PO ... Luke ... Aaron," I answered. "I'll be free after I wrap up with them though. Hopefully, it won't take all day."

Brianna nodded and kissed me on the lips before pulling away and leaning against the sink. I stepped into the closet and started to get dressed.

"You seem like you've been under a lot of stress lately ... is it work-related?" she asked.

I hesitated before answering her. Although it seemed like a simple yes or no answer, it wasn't. Yes, a lot of my stress had come from the changes going on with work. My dad being absent, Aaron being in charge, Blue's death, and the threat of the Pitt twins all were contributing factors to the stress that weighed on me. That wasn't all though. Even though I cared about Brianna and was entertaining her seriously at the moment, I was still a little stressed about the way things ended with Shannon. I couldn't share that with Brianna. As far as I knew, she didn't know anything about Shannon. The remaining things she left behind had were moved to one of the guest rooms, and I told Brianna that it belonged to one of my sisters.

After pulling on my jeans I stepped back into the bathroom.

"Pretty much," I answered. "There's a lot going on with work lately. Not having my dad and my brother around hasn't been easy."

"Would you ever give it all up?" she asked.

I looked at Brianna with a confused frown.

"What?"

"I mean ... have you ever considered what your life would be like if you did something else?" Brianna asked. She reached for my arm and pulled me closer to her. "What if you left all that street shit alone and lived a regular ass life? Got a regular job with a regular woman and settled down and had some regular ass kids. Is that something you would consider?"

I kissed her on the lips. "I ain't opposed to settling down. Eventually, I may want some kids too, but all that other shit … I don't know about that," I answered her. "To be honest … that's never even crossed my mind. This is all that I know. My father's been doing this shit since before I was born. I don't think I ever considered making a living any other way."

Brianna nodded in acknowledgment of my statement, and I saw a hint of disappointment in her eyes.

"Is that a problem?" I asked with a confused frown. I never hid who I was from her. She always knew about the life that I lived.

Brianna shook her head. "No. I know who you are," she said as she turned away from me and started to brush her teeth.

I thought about asking what was on her mind but then thought against it. I needed to finish getting ready so that I could be at the meeting on time. We could finish our discussion later. I brushed my teeth as well and finished putting on my clothes. Brianna was pulling on her jeans when I stepped back into my bedroom.

"What do you have planned for the day?" I asked.

"Nothing major," Brianna answered with a shrug of her shoulders. "I'll be around."

"Cool. I'll hit you up when I'm finished," I said. "We can go to dinner and finish that conversation if you want."

"Sure," Brianna said with a weak smile as she slipped into her jacket and grabbed her car keys.

I grabbed my things and exited the house behind her. I was interested in finding out what her problem was later.

JADA

"How are you feeling, Mrs. Mercer?" Sophia asked from the third row of the Escalade.

I looked over my shoulder and smiled at my mother-in-law while she sat behind me. "I am over the moon," I answered with a smile a mile wide.

Sophia patted my shoulder and I turned around and settled into my seat. Aaron was holding my right hand while he spoke on his cell phone. I looked down at my left hand, admiring the diamond wedding band that complimented my engagement ring. Together the two rings made an impressive fourteen-carat total weight wedding set. While Aaron gave me with the attention-grabbing set of diamonds, he had opted for a way more modest Cartier plain platinum wedding band. As our driver, Scott, started to pull away from the courthouse, Aaron ended his call.

"Hey man, everyone is waiting for us. You can go straight to the house," he instructed Scott. He turned towards me. Lifting the hand that he held, he kissed it and said, "I told you I couldn't wait to make you the new Mrs. Mercer."

"I see. You didn't waste any time," I joked. "Seriously though, I'm happy. Our little one will be here before we know it, and I'm happy that our family is official."

"Me too," he said with a smile.

At thirty-four weeks pregnant, we only had a little over a month before our child was born. I was getting more excited each day. In the two weeks since Aaron had suggested we have our courthouse wedding, things were settling down. I was preparing to hand the day-to-day operations of my businesses off to Ayanna and my managers while I prepped for the birth of the baby. My father would be returning home from California in a few weeks. Cameron and Aaron were finally on better terms. Things even appeared to be going smoother for Aaron with work, and I had hoped that we would soon be able to ease up on all the security. However that had not happened yet, and

Harold and Vic were in the truck with us as we made our way back home.

Our courthouse ceremony had been quick and quiet with Sophia as our only witness. Our families and a few close friends were waiting at the house to celebrate our nuptials with a catered dinner party. Soon, we pulled through the gate to the neighborhood and up to our home. We were welcomed with hugs from our guests as we entered the house. Vanessa worked with a high-profile party planner to create the set up for our gathering. The furniture was removed from the great room with tables brought in to seat our guests comfortably. While we started to get settled and seated, I was able to speak with my brother.

"Congrats Sis," Cameron said after giving me a hug.

"Thank you. I'm glad you made it," I said. I quickly glanced around the room. "Are you alone? I thought you were bringing your new girlfriend?"

Cameron shook his head. "I originally planned on it but changed my mind. Knowing that you and Shannon are still cool I thought there was a chance she would be here tonight. I wanted to avoid that drama."

"I invited her," I told him as I looked around the room again, "but she's not here. Maybe she's not ready to face you."

"It's cool." Cameron shrugged his shoulders. "Today is about you and your boy."

"Your brother-in-law," I said with a smile.

"Whatever," Cameron laughed. "I'm happy that you're happy. I mean that. You deserve it."

"I appreciate that, Cameron. Thank you."

We all took our seats and started to eat. Vanessa took all the planning off my hands and executed a perfect event. As I looked around the room at everyone who joined us in celebration, my heart was full. Again, I marveled at how much could change in a year's time. After surviving what was arguably one of the toughest years of my life, I made it to the other side to what was looking like one of the best years of my life.

Our dinner party lasted well into the evening, with toasts from his parents, Luke, and Vanessa. The house finally cleared out around midnight, except for Aaron's immediate family members that would be staying with us for one more day. After a shower, I was in our bathroom, dressed in my nightgown and washing the makeup from my face. Aaron appeared in the doorway while I patted my face dry with a towel.

"You know I really can't thank you enough for pushing up the wedding," he said. "I don't think you know how much it means to me."

I turned towards him with a smile.

"It was a pretty easy sell when you told me the budget would be unlimited for the ceremony next year," I responded. I held up my hand to admire my rings. "Besides, I got some pretty cool jewelry to enjoy in the meantime."

Aaron laughed as he stepped further into the bathroom, pulling me into his arms.

"For real. I just wanted to start our married life as soon as possible. I want us to have as much time as the good Lord will allow," Aaron said, looking into my eyes.

"Babe, this is a forever thing. We've got all the time in the world."

"I hope you're right, mama," he said with a serious look in his eyes. "With the life that we live ... you know that anything can happen at any time. I love you beyond reason, and I would never leave you on purpose. I want to grow old and gray with you, but Jada ... with what my father and I do for a living ... there are no guarantees."

Something about his tone of voice and the look in his eyes caused a chill to run up my spine. I knew him. Looking into his eyes, I knew there was something he wasn't telling me. As curious as I was, I didn't want the answers at that moment.

"Baby, that's a pretty heavy conversation for our wedding night," I said to him.

I took a step away from him, untying my robe to reveal a white lace and silk maternity negligee. Aaron looked me up and down with a pleased smile on his face. He shook his head slightly but maintained his wide smile and placed his hands on my hips.

"All that talking I was just doing ... I'm sure I could find a better use for my mouth right now," he said before kissing my lips.

"That's what I thought," I said as I took his hand and headed into our bedroom.

SHANNON

My plan was to get in and out the house as soon as possible. Jada invited me to the post-wedding dinner party at her and Aaron's house, but I chose not to attend. I knew that Cameron was going to be there. Regardless of how he felt about his sister's husband, I knew there was no way he would miss something like that. That gave me the perfect opportunity to go by his house and grab the rest of my belongings. Alicia offered to come with me, but I didn't need any help. I just wanted to grab my things and officially close the chapter of my life that included Cameron Reid.

I pulled into the neighborhood and quickly made my way to his street. I parked about two or three houses down from the house we once shared. I stared at the driveway in disbelief while I saw the familiar BMW that belonged to his side bitch. I gripped the steering wheel in anger. I had barely been out of his house for a month, and he had already moved that bitch into my spot. I still had clothes hanging in the closet and toiletries in the bathroom, and yet her car had made its home in the driveway. I shook my head and took a deep breath to calm myself. He was stupid – so fucking stupid. He deserved exactly what was coming his way.

For a brief moment, I considered turning my engine back on and leaving. I thought about disappearing and going somewhere to lick my wounds in private. Throughout the course of our relationship, Cameron threw more than enough money my way. I never pictured things would end the way it did, but luckily, I was smart enough to save money he had given me. I had more than enough cash to go somewhere and get my head together. Prior to coming to his house, I had no intentions of interfering in the situation that was brewing with his new lady.

But something wouldn't let me disappear so quietly.

Something about seeing her car in the driveway, thinking about her lying in the bed that I slept in every night, and taking my place made me completely change my mind. I exited the car and crossed the street, making my way to the house. Cameron had not bothered to take my key or even change the locks.

What a dumbass.

I unlocked the door and let myself into the house. Closing the door behind me, I stood in the foyer. I was sure that she heard the door open and close. I turned the alarm off and waited at the bottom of the stairs. Thinking that Cameron had returned home, I figured it would only be a few moments before she joined me.

Sure enough, I heard footsteps coming down the hallway not even five seconds later. "Cam, I thought you were going to be gone until –"

Dressed in lingerie and a long silk robe, she paused at the top of the stairs when she realized I was not Cameron. Her eyes darted around the foyer. I could only assume that she was trying to locate the nearest firearm.

"Relax," I told her. "I'm not even here on any animosity type shit. My anger isn't directed towards you."

She relaxed but only slightly. She tied the belt of her robe around her waist. "Shannon, what are you doing here?"

"I guess I shouldn't be surprised that you know my name," I said with a smirk.

"I know all about you," she said. "Most importantly I know that you and Cameron are done. So, I don't know what you're doing here, but you should probably leave. He won't be back for a while."

"I know where he is. His sister got married today. I just came over get the rest of my shit out of his house," I said. "Since you're here though, maybe we should talk. Especially since I know all about you, and who you really are."

I watched as her face tightened into a frown.

"What are you talking about?"

I laughed and shook my head. This whole situation was completely unbelievable. I looked directly in her eyes and said, "I think you know exactly what I'm talking about, Agent Franklin."

She froze.

"DEA, is it?" I asked with a satisfied grin. She didn't respond so I continued. "Like I said, my anger isn't directed towards you. Why don't you come down here so we can talk? I might have some useful information to help you make your case. After all, isn't that why you've been fucking my man for the past several months? You're trying to build a federal case against him, right?"

Special Agent Kendra Franklin hesitated at the top of the stairs for a few more moments before making her way down to join me.

AARON

*L*uke and I laughed at PO's joke while were walked out of the warehouse. Another profitable and quiet week had ended, and we were all glad to be done with work for the night. The warm, May evening air was inviting as I stood in the parking lot watching Luke lock everything up.

"Aye, man, Nakia doesn't get back up here until tomorrow," Luke said. "Y'all trying to step out tonight?"

"I'm down, but you know Aaron's on baby watch and shit," PO joked. "He's probably got to get home to the wife."

I laughed, but PO was right. Jada was thirty-eight weeks pregnant with her doctor advising that she could go into labor at any moment. Even though I knew she probably wouldn't care, I did not feel like going to the club. I could get a drink in the comfort of my own home while relaxing with my pregnant wife.

"Yeah, man. As much as I would like to kick back with y'all, I think I'm going to call it a night and go see my baby," I said.

Luke laughed and shook his head at me. "This guy," he said to PO. "Man, I could tell you some stories about the way he used to run through women when he was in these streets."

"Hey, man! Chill," I laughed, holding a finger up to my lips. "I don't know what you're talking about. I've always been a one-woman man."

Luke turned towards PO while shaking his head. "Don't believe the lies this nigga is trying to tell you," he said. "I'm glad Jada came along and calmed his ass down."

PO laughed and shrugged his shoulders. "Even the biggest hoes change when they meet the right one," he said.

"Goddamn," I laughed. "Why are y'all going in on me?"

The three of us shared a laugh and walked towards our vehicles. I pressed the remote to unlock the Maserati when I felt my phone start to vibrate. I expected it to be Jada asking me to bring home her latest craving, but I was surprised to see Regina calling me.

"What's up, Gigi?" I answered the call.

"Aaron, dad is in the hospital," she said with emotion in her voice.

It was rare for Regina to show any kind of emotion. I wasn't sure if I had heard her correctly.

"What?"

"He's in the hospital," she repeated. "I don't really know what all is going on. Mom just asked me to call you. He's been dealing with a cold for a while, and he started coughing up blood the other day, so mama made him go to the doctor. They think it might be cancer."

"Cancer? What the fuck?" I asked.

The laughter from PO and Luke's side conversation stopped and they looked at me with concern.

"I don't know, Aaron," she said. "They're still running tests. We don't have any answers right now."

"Alright. Give me a few minutes," I said. "I'm going to call you back shortly."

I ended the call, shaking my head as I scrolled to Jada's number in my contacts.

"What's going on, Black?" Luke asked.

"My dad's in the hospital," I answered without looking directly at him or PO.

I pressed the button to dial Jada's number. She answered quickly.

"Hey ... I was just about to call you," she said. "Daniella just called me. Are you headed to the airport?"

"I was about to head home," I answered her. "Of course I'm concerned about my father, but your water could break at any moment."

"It's okay. Ayanna and Vanessa are in town, and if anything happens, I know you'll head right back up here," Jada said. "I promise I'll be fine. Go check on your dad. Your mom and sisters are very worried."

"Jada, are you sure?" I asked. "I don't really feel comfortable leaving you right now."

"Harold and Vic are here, and my sister is one call away," she said. "A flight from Miami to Atlanta is only ninety minutes. You can get back up here quickly if I need you, but I will be fine."

"Alright. I'll call you when I get down there," I said. "I love you."

"I love you too."

I ended my call with Jada and spoke briefly with Luke and PO. Luke drove me to the airport where I caught the first flight down to Miami. I was at the hospital within a couple of hours. When I reached his room, my mother was there alone while my father slept.

"Mijo," she greeted me with a hug and a kiss on the cheek.

"Where's Dani and Gigi?" I asked, sitting down in a chair next to her.

"I told them they could go home," she said. "It's late. There's nothing they can do right now."

I nodded in acknowledgment.

As I listened to my mother's update, I knew that there wasn't much she could do at that moment either. She looked tired and stressed, but I knew that suggesting she go home and get some rest would be a waste of my time. She wasn't going to leave his side. The suspicion was that my father had lung cancer. X-rays and a CT scan from earlier in the day had revealed lesions on his lungs. We were awaiting the final results from a biopsy and further information in regard to what stage he was facing to determine treatment plans.

My head was spinning with the information my mother gave me. I rarely saw my father sick so the realization of what we were facing felt like unchartered territory. If my father was facing a potentially terminal, illness, I knew it would have a significant impact on our family. In addition, I couldn't help but think about the way it could affect business. I was being prepared to take over for him, but that wasn't supposed to happen so soon. Things were finally starting to calm down for me – just in time for the birth of my child. I wasn't sure if I was ready to step up and take over for my dad with the baby on the way and everything else going on. I hoped that the doctors' assumption was incorrect.

Two days later, suspicions were confirmed. My father had stage 3 lung cancer. After going over the treatment plan, the doctors were preparing to release him from the hospital. I was pacing the floor in the waiting room scrolling through a few text messages when my Uncle Nate approached me. He had a serious look on his face.

"Hey, Black," he greeted me.

"What's up, Unc?"

Something made me feel that he was bringing more bad news.

"When is Julian going to be back in Atlanta?" he asked.

I shrugged my shoulders. "Day after tomorrow I believe," I answered. "What's going on?"

Nate released a deep sigh as he slid his hands into his pockets.

"We've got another problem in Atlanta. I need you to head back down there," he answered.

"Now?" I asked with a frown. "Pops is about to be released."

"Now," he replied. "I'll stay with your parents. Gigi and I are more than capable of making sure your father gets settled at home."

"What's going on?" I asked again.

"Black, the Pitt twins aren't the only problem that Julian Reid's team is facing right now. After the fallout with Caleb Bridges and KS9, the mayor and local law enforcement haven't been sticking their neck out to protect Julian like usual. I just got word that the DEA has actually been trying to build a case for several months," Uncle Nate said as he pulled his cell phone out of his pocket. "They apparently have an agent that's been undercover nosing around the organization. Does this person look familiar to you?"

I looked at the picture on his phone in disbelief as I recognized the person in the photo to be Cameron's lady friend. The same lady friend that he had messed around with for months. The lady friend that he had in our East Atlanta house in the middle of a goddamn meeting. My jaw clenched in anger as I felt the pressure of a headache building. Cameron was so careless over the last year. There was no telling what this DEA agent knew. I didn't know all the specifics, but she knew where we operated business. She had seen our faces. Hell, she knew our names.

"That's the chick Cameron has been messing around with for months," I finally said.

"Your father's jet is ready to take you back to Atlanta," my uncle stated. "I already called Luke. He's going to pick you up from the airport. I need you to go handle business."

"I got it," I said as we shared a brief hug. "Tell my parents I'll call them tomorrow."

I headed out of the hospital's front entrance where my driver, Julio, was already waiting to take me to the airport. On the way, I called Luke who told me that he already had the East Atlanta house emptied and wiped clean of any evidence that we were ever there. The lease was secured using fraudulent information, so we were hopeful that there was no paper trail leading to us.

"Where's Cameron?" I asked.

"I don't know. I haven't been able to get in contact with him," Luke answered. "Do you want me to go over there?"

"Nah. I don't want you anywhere near him," I responded. "After you pick me up from the airport, we need to get in contact with PO. We need to start shutting down all the other spots like the warehouse and the tire shop. We need to switch everything up."

"I hear you, Black. We might not be able to save Cameron right now, but we can try to protect everyone else," Luke said.

When the jet landed, I headed right for Luke's truck. I hopped in and he pulled out of the parking lot of the small commercial airport.

"Where are we heading?" I asked him while I took my phone off of airplane mode.

"Back to my place," Luke said. He navigated his way towards the interstate. "PO told me to let him know when we made it over there, and he would be on his way. We need to try and find a way out of the shit storm your brother-in-law created."

I nodded in acknowledgment but frowned at my phone when I noticed that I had a number of missed voicemails from Vic. It should have been a normal, quiet Monday evening. If he was blowing my phone up, something was wrong.

Noticing my facial expression, Luke asked, "What's wrong, Black?"

"I don't know," I answered.

Right as I was about to dial Vic's number, he called me again.

"Vic, what's going on?"

"We can't find Jada, boss," he said in a frustrated tone.

"What?" I shouted into the phone. "What the fuck do you mean you can't find her?"

"She left the house when I was in the bathroom," he said.

"Where the fuck is Harold?" I shouted.

"He was running a little late, but he's at the house now," Vic responded. "We checked with the front gate at the neighborhood. She left by herself in her truck. No one grabbed her but –"

"That's not the point! She's not supposed to be unattended," I cut him off. "Now you're telling me that you don't know where she is?"

"She's not answering the phone," Vic said. "Boss, we are –"

I hung up and called Jada's phone. She didn't answer. Knowing that she left our home voluntarily was only a minor relief. The thought of her being thirty-eight weeks pregnant and roaming the streets by herself at night did not sit right with me, especially when the Pitt twins could possibly still be in Atlanta. It had been a whirlwind twelve hours. From receiving confirmation of my father's cancer to hearing word that the DEA was on our tail and my wife slipped past her security, my mind was racing. I needed to make contact with Jada and make sure she was okay.

CAMERON

It was a quiet Monday evening. After wrapping up a few work-related things, I grabbed dinner and headed home. I ate my chicken wings in front of the television in the living room with an ice-cold beer while watching a basketball game and enjoying my solitude. Luke tried to reach me a few times, but I ignored his call. I didn't feel like being bothered. In a few days my father would be home, and I hoped he would resume his role of power. When Julian Reid returned to Atlanta, I was done answering to Lucas Malone and Aaron Mercer.

Brianna sent me a text earlier in the day letting me know that she planned to stop by and wanted to make sure I would be home. It would be the first time I saw her in a few days. She was a little distant for the last month or so since I told her I had no intentions of changing my career path. If she was going to be with me, she would have to accept me for who I was – the rightful heir to all my father had built. If she had a problem with that, she could be replaced too – just like Shannon. Somewhere during the broadcast of a west coast basketball game, I started to doze off on the couch and decided to head upstairs. I assumed Brianna changed her mind about coming over. I didn't think twice about it. I had other things on my mind. I was eagerly awaiting my father's return, and I didn't mind getting a peaceful night of sleep in my bed alone. I climbed into the bed and was asleep within minutes.

I don't know how long I actually slept before I was awakened by the disturbance outside of my home. In my mind, I think I knew exactly what was happening the moment I heard the sound of helicopters hovering overhead. That's why it was no surprise when I heard my door being kicked in moments later. I laid on my back in my bed staring at the ceiling while I waited. It only took a few seconds before I heard the footsteps from the heavy boots coming down the hallway heading for my room. I didn't even flinch when they ran into my room with guns drawn and flashlights.

"Get on the ground!"

"Put your hands behind your back!"

I heard someone call me by my full legal name before two agents grabbed me from the bed, throwing me face down onto the floor. I remained calm. If there was one thing I actually learned from my father, it was to remain calm in situations like this.

"You have the right to remain silent. Anything you say can and will be used against you in a court of law …"

I didn't plan on saying a word. I remained stone-faced while my hands were cuffed behind my back and I was brought up to my feet. I was led out of the house into the night air towards one of the waiting law enforcement vehicles. Keeping my mouth shut, I tuned out all of the noise surrounding me while I went over the events of the last year wondering how I had gotten to this point. I was reckless enough to allow individuals like Carlos and Dre into the fold – individuals that proved they could not be trusted. I wondered if Dre was the reason for the night's turn of events.

While one of the agents opened the back door to the vehicle, I saw a familiar face standing next to another unmarked car. All I could do was shake my head in disbelief when my eyes locked with Brianna's … or whatever her real name was. When my eyes lowered to the letters "DEA" written across her jacket, I knew I was fucked.

I had spent so much time worried about the wrong things – the wrong enemy. The Pitts didn't have shit on the Feds.

Only heaven knew how I was going to get out of this one.

Jada

I could hear my cell phone ringing from the bedroom while I finished using the master bathroom at my condo. It was almost midnight. Very few people would have been trying to reach me at that time of night. I assumed it was Harold or Vic. They had blown up my phone since realizing I left the house. I got bored earlier and decided to do a little bit of work even though I was supposed to be on maternity leave. I needed a couple of hard copies of financial reports that I left in my condo. When I was ready to leave the house, Vic had been in the bathroom.

So, I took the liberty of driving myself. It was only fifteen minutes away from the house. I planned on being in and out and back home in no time. I washed my hands and dried them on a hand towel when I heard my phone ring again. From the ringtone, I knew that Aaron was trying to reach me for the second time. I already missed one of his calls when I was using the bathroom, so I quickly jogged back to my bedroom to retrieve my phone from my purse.

"Hey, baby," I greeted him with a smile.

"Jada, where are you?" he shouted through the phone.

The smile dropped from my face. There was a sense of urgency and panic in his voice that replaced his usual calm tone.

"I just came by the condo real quick. I needed –"

"Without your security? Dammit, Jada!"

"Babe," I responded. "I just needed to grab –"

"It don't care what you thought you needed. You shouldn't have gone anywhere without Harold or Vic! Get out of there now!" he shouted. "I'm on my way. Wait for me in the lobby!"

"What?" I asked confused. "Why are you back in town?"

"Jada, get downstairs. *NOW!*"

He hung up before I could ask any more questions. I knew better than to try and call him back. Whatever was going on must have been serious. I quickly grabbed my things and headed for the door. I swung it open and was startled to find someone standing on the other side – an unfamiliar woman staring back at me. She was tall and attractive, but the ice-cold glare in her eyes was unnerving.

"Can I help you?" I asked.

She smirked before responding. The malice in her eyes remained. "I'm actually surprised that you're here," she said.

"I think you have the wrong place," I said, as I tried to step past her and close my door.

She didn't move. She continued to stand in place, blocking me from entering the hallway. Annoyed, I frowned.

"Like I was saying, Jada … I'm surprised you came over here. I can't believe that hubby of yours allowed you to go anywhere without your security detail," she laughed. She pushed my shoulder, causing me to stumble backwards into my foyer. "He's still out of town, right? This should be a lot easier than I thought."

I struggled to keep my footing while she stepped into the condo and closed the door.

"What the –"

She silenced me when she pulled a gun from her jacket pocket and pointed it at me. She used her other hand to retrieve her cell phone and place a call.

"Yeah Mikey. She's up here. Unit 1236. The door's unlocked."

Mikey? I thought to myself. There were very few grown men I knew that were called Mikey.

Holy shit.

I overheard enough conversations throughout the years to know of a Mikey. Mikey Pitt. That would have made the woman in front of me … his twin …

"Michaela?" I asked.

She smirked again but kept her gun aimed in my direction. "I heard you were the smart one," she responded. "Julian's baby girl. His pride and joy … also his weakness. You obviously weren't smart enough to bring your security with you, but I'd have to be an idiot to think that you would be going anywhere without a weapon of your own."

Behind her the door opened and closed as her twin brother, Mikey, entered the condo. He locked the door before approaching his sister's side. Michaela never took her eyes off of me as she spoke again.

"Drop your bag slowly and kick it over to me."

I did as I was told, slowly placing my Louis Vuitton Never-full tote on the floor and using my foot to slide it towards the twins. Mikey bent down and quickly sifted through the purse. He pulled out my 40 caliber Smith & Wesson and showed it to Michaela. They both nodded in admiration.

"Nice," Michaela said.

"This a big ass gun for a girl," Mikey said.

Michaela rolled her eyes at her brother. "Nigga, shut the hell up and sit her ass at the table," she motioned towards my dining room.

It quickly became clear to that Michaela was the one in charge. With my gun still in his hand, Mikey shrugged his shoulders and sighed. As he started to walk in my direction, I backpedaled slowly, but Mikey firmly grabbed my arm and pushed me towards the table. He pulled a chair out and forced me to sit.

"Place your hands on the table," he spat. "Lay 'em flat."

With Mikey pointing my own gun at me, Michaela finally lowered her weapon by her side. She casually walked around my common area, seemingly admiring my furnishings. I pressed my hands flat on the table in front of me. I took a deep breath to calm my nerves. I didn't need to let them know that I was rattled.

"You've got a very nice place here. Top of the line décor ... excellent views," Michaela said. "Too bad you won't get to enjoy it for much longer."

"What is this about?" I asked evenly.

From what I knew, they were the best contract killers in the business. I had no idea why they would be after me or anyone in my family for that matter. My dad hadn't even been around to piss anyone off. Mikey didn't answer me, and Michaela gave me a sideways glance.

"It's a wonder that your family has built the empire that you have, because you are all so incredibly stupid," she said. "By your family ... I'm referring to the one you were born into. Not the Mercers."

Her response did nothing to answer my question, and I continued to stare at her.

"Do you know who I am?" she asked.

"Michaela Pitt."

"No, honey," she said. "I mean do you know who I am connected to? Do you know who my family is ... or *was* for that matter?"

"No," I answered. "You two are practically invisible. No one knows any personal details about you."

She shrugged her shoulders. "Maybe that's why your family made the mistake of killing our cousin."

Cousin? I didn't know who the hell she was talking about. No one had ever made mention of the Pitt twins having family. Furthermore, my dad and brothers rarely involved me in the details of their operation. I had no clue who she was referring to. Usually If my dad or Cameron killed someone, I would have been the last person to know. I looked down at my hands still pressed on my dining room table. I had no interest in learning the details of their family tree. I needed Aaron to show up – fast.

Michaela looked towards her brother and shook her head. "Awww ... she had no idea that Caleb was our cousin," she said.

Caleb? My stomach turned at the mention of his name. Caleb Bridges was the cause of almost everything that had gone wrong a year and a half prior. His actions caused the death of my brother Deuce, Kelvin Massey – a childhood friend, and the irreparable rift in my relationship with Israel. Now he indirectly caused the current situation that I was facing. Caleb's death apparently sent the Hit twins on a personal revenge mission that ultimately led them to my front door. My heart dropped at the realization that if my husband didn't show up soon it would be lights out for me and our unborn child.

"What?" Michaela asked. "You don't have any more questions for me or my brother?"

I shook my head but never raised my eyes to meet hers. *Where the hell was Aaron?*

Michaela rolled her eyes in disgust. "Get her ass up and walk her back to the bathroom," she instructed her brother. "Let's get this shit over with so we can finally get the hell out of Atlanta."

Once again, Mikey followed his sister's orders and snatched me out of my chair. We had only taken two steps towards the bedroom when the front door swung open. Mikey and Michaela both turned towards the entrance of my condo with their weapons raised. Aaron and Luke were standing there, guns drawn as well. Mikey released his hold on my arm and completely turned to face Aaron and Luke. Everything happened so quickly.

I heard someone shout, "Jada, get down!"

I quickly dropped down to the ground.

Then the gunshots started.

Mikey took his eyes off of Aaron and Luke to aim my gun at me again. Unable to watch, I closed my eyes. Only a split second passed before I heard Mikey fire my gun. Two bullets entered my body right before I heard Mikey's body drop on the floor beside me.

More gunshots.

The sound of another body hitting the floor.

Running footsteps.

Then silence.

I could feel the blood seeping from my wounds. I fought to open my eyes and assess the damage, but I couldn't. My head was heavy, and my body was weak.

"Fuck!" I heard Luke shout. *"Fuck!"*

I heard footsteps move towards me and hands on my shoulders, shaking me.

"Come on, Jada," Luke's voice called to me. "Get up! Open your eyes!"

But I couldn't get up, and I couldn't open my eyes. I had no control over my body. As I literally felt the life draining from me, all I could think about was my husband and our unborn child. *Where was Aaron?* I appreciated Luke's concern, but why was he the one attending to me?

Why wasn't my husband at my side?

Why ...

ABOUT THE AUTHOR

Michelle Elaine is an author of African American and Urban fiction and romance. Born and raised in Atlanta, GA, she still resides in the metro area with her husband and sons. She has always been passionate about storytelling and character creation/development. This passion led to several short stories and development of plots and characters before she completed her first book, "A Good Girl & A Down South Millionaire". Visit her website and join her mailing list to stay in the know on the latest releases, etc.

Other ways to stay connected:
　　Facebook – Author Michelle Elaine
　　Instagram – authormichelleelaine
　　Website – www.michelleelainebooks.com
　　Email – michelleelainebooks@outlook.com

Made in the USA
Monee, IL
25 May 2021

69450564R00132

Hoodfellas II:
American Gangster

By

Richard Jeanty

RJ Publications, LLC

Newark, New Jersey

The characters and events in this book are fictitious. Any resemblance to actual persons, living or dead is purely coincidental.

RJ Publications
richjeanty@yahoo.com
www.rjpublications.com
Copyright © 2010 by Richard Jeanty
All Rights Reserved
ISBN 0981999808
978-0981999807

Printed in the Canada

March 2010

1 2 3 4 5 6 7 8 9 10

APR 2010